YOUR *Soul* IS *Ours*

TANYA LYNN

Paperback ISBN: 978-1-7380127-4-9

Dedication

Dear Reader

This story took hold of me after an intense therapy session. The characters wouldn't let me go and kept talking until I wrote. I know that not every person who has a narcissistic mother has the same type of abuse or behaviours, and I don't want you to think I discredit other forms of abuse.

I see you. I'm incredibly proud of the person you've become. I think in some ways we just want to hear that we matter, that someone gives a shit. Because it's hard when your family sucks.

The aspect of mental health services in this book may seem like a parody. I don't take mental health lightly and I joke about the services offered because otherwise I think I would give up. I know that there is a crisis everywhere, but through my own experiences, this is how I see the mental health system that the government provides through my own perceptions.

Mental illness affects us all differently. What I experience can be similar or vastly different from what you experience, even if we have the same diagnosis. Everything is valid—what you feel and what others may feel. Just because you've met someone with depression doesn't mean you've met everyone with depression.

This book has a self-harm component, if that is triggering, don't read it. I care about your streak of no self-harm more than I would ever care about a book sale. I know that fighting a battle that no one can see, that feels wrong to even talk about, can be isolating and heartbreaking. I'm proud of however many days you have achieved without self-harming.

Every instance in this book is a recount from my memory. I do know what the silent war feels like, the shame, and how you can never quite get the same high as you did when you started.

We take it a day at a time, and hope for the best. I'm fucking proud of you.

This book deals with suicide. Again, I can't say it loud enough that if you will be triggered, please don't read it. You are fucking important, and you should be here with us, topside.

I dedicate this book to all the mental health survivors. May we trudge along and continue living this life thing because, taking the forever dirt nap, if we get sent to Cavum Terra, it would be fucking horrific.

Make sure you check the other TWs and take care of yourself.

This book took a lot from me to write, though it was cathartic at times. In other ways, it destroyed me. Trauma sucks. Let's be honest, Trauma sucks! And when we stir it all up, it sucks more. This book took a part of my soul, many of my tears, and even a piece of my cold, dead heart.

Tanya Lynn.

Trigger Warnings

Suicide
Medically assisted suicide
Suicidal thoughts
Self-harm (cutting)
Death
Murder
Teeth pulling
Some mention of torture
Blood
Mention of past child abuse
Narcissistic parent abuse
Mental health services
Dystopian society vibes in regards to mental health services
Fantasy realm (where you go if you commit suicide)
Shadow demons that torment you in the realm
Mental illness: Anxiety, depression, CPTSD

Stalking
Gun use
Mass shooting
Talk of drug use
Cigarettes
House fire
Death by house fire
Graphic Violence
Blood play
Knife play
Unprotected sex
Hand necklaces
Pierced penis
Explicit sex scenes
Explicit language

Prologue

Cavum Terra

The haze across the realm has settled since the new arrivals, orange, and red colours stretch across the sky, not a cloud in sight.

"Do you think they're ready for this?" Tanca asks me.

"They never are. The change period for both souls and demons is large." I walk down the winding beaten path to our cabins. You would expect great rulers to have better dwellings, but we manage.

"The humans are upset, the anguish has started, and I doubt that anger will be far behind," Giso tells me as she joins me on the walk.

"We can't go to Earth and give a presentation on what happens when you kill yourself. It's unethical. They have to learn the hard way," I say.

As we reach the main cabin, I look over the manifesto of the souls that have found their way here. The demons that have haunted their minds for far too long are on the same line. There are many this time.

"We will have to mind the demons. It will be the first time they are in physical form with their humans. We don't want any serious injuries or death. They'll have to give them time to heal," Giso says quietly.

"We need a better method, Berimund. The chaos and emotions create a darkness in the air that pisses me off," Tanca says.

I raise my hands in the air. "It's only for a few days. The darkness tapers off when they realize this is the way life will be for them."

"I'm surprised by the amount. It is more this time than we have ever had," Giso says, twisting her blonde hair around her finger.

"The death, the tragedy, the hunger and trauma, the atrocious people running rampant... I wouldn't want to live there," I reply.

"We'll brief the last group on how to help the newcomers best. They have fought until hope was lost and learned that it's easier to let the demons win. The demons are a heavy burden to carry on Earth, but damn near impossible here," Tanca tells me.

"We're not briefing anyone. The unknown is for the best." Both of them look at me with disgust, as we head for our own cabins. I've been here for over a millennium and don't see things changing for the better. Every new soul brings forth physical manifestations of the demons within their minds. I cannot, in good conscience, move to Earth and deliver the message that yielding to one's mental demons will lead to a physical war in the afterlife. My only option is to leave it be and hope for the best.

One

Marla

"*And she'd just hide in the background like a beaten dog.*" My mother's words haunt my thoughts, the memories swimming like fish through my mind, flashing throughout the day.

I stand at the back of the mental health centre. The fine for disobeying keeps me here, although I'm tired of it. Having mandated mental health services that never really help is soul-crushing. I come here every other day as ordered by my doctor, and skipping it completely would cause me to be taken away to die at the hands of the man. If I'm going to die, it'll be on my own terms.

I'm a bit confused about the concept, but it seems like the government holds the ability to judge someone's right to live based on their role as a productive member of society. The historical mental health crisis reached such alarming proportions it jeopardized the entire country, compelling the government to take this action. Breaking any rules will cause severe consequences - fines, prison time, or both. Despite their promises of progress, I can't help but feel like we're all mere puppets, performing on a stage for the man.

The centre is monochrome, with white walls, white floors and, black rubber baseboards. Old newspapers and magazines lay on the tables. Posters cover the walls, talking about mental illness, ways to reach out, numbers to call. The line is moving slowly, detailing its length. People in the room have a vacant look in their eyes, standing around until they can finally fill out the forms. Stale coffee and body odour swim through the air, along with the stench of disinfectants. My head spins with the mingling scents, sweat beads on my brow and my stomach roils.

According to the doctor forms, if you reach the front of the line, you fill out the paperwork, and if you pass intake, the government doles out six hours of sessions because you'll be done and miraculously cured in that time. Three days a week I show up, wait for the allowed time, and then leave. I've never gotten close enough to have an intake, instead I'm stuck with the herd. People and faces come and go, disappearing with time. Sometimes faces fade because they didn't come, they rejected the help and were sent to jail or death. Others get through and do their time. The government doesn't give a shit. The money they fund is so insignificant that it hardly makes a difference to those in need. Our souls are so dark that the world cannot bear their weight.

Mental health services are an illusion of someone giving a fuck about you. With the money they would save, they should just hand us all a rope, a bottle of pills or a sharp blade. But they won't, calling it a tragedy. More times than not, they decide who isn't a functioning member of society and those people never return.

"Such horseshit. How many days have you been here?" a voice asks from beside me. I swivel my head but keep my back pressed against the wall, leaning on my other leg. I see him, a dude who wants to make small talk.

"I come three times a week."

"Do you think they'll save our lives?" he asks, and I glance in his direction to take him in. Black boots, black jeans, black shirt, and dark hair cut in an edgy way. The shaved sides show off the black spacers in his ears. Tattoos cover his neck and the designs spiral out from the sleeves of his shirt.

"Nah, no one is coming to save our lives. Apparently we're supposed to do that ourselves."

His low snicker takes me off guard. I've never met anyone who can laugh about this shit. If you laugh at the demons in your head, they quiet slightly, if only for a minute, like it embarrasses them that you don't care.

"Who wants to send you here?" I whisper, not wanting to call attention to myself. Those reminders traipse through my mind. If my mother knew I was here, she'd lose her mind.

"All the experts." His dark brown eyes look into mine, but the sarcastic edge in his voice doesn't pass me by. I slide down the wall. I didn't plan on sitting on the floor, but my sore legs demand it.

"Who sends you here?" he asks, sinking down beside me. His pants rattle as he sits, and I wonder what's in his pockets.

"The experts. The letters show up weekly." I cross my legs, sitting criss-cross applesauce.

"I've never gotten letters," he says.

This is the most social interaction I've had in months, unless you count the endless calls of torture from family. This guy has the vibe of a red flag. His style is douchebag mixed with grunge, like a fuckboy who doesn't want to be pretty, who has a harder edge than he should.

"Attention, the centre is closing for the day. You can come back on your next appointed day to get access to the services again." The announcement blares over the P.A. system from the woman behind the plexiglass holding a microphone. She gives the fake-ass smile they do every time I'm here.

"Fuck," he says from beside me. I glance at him before I push myself off the floor.

"Will you be here tomorrow?" he asks. I shrug as I walk through the procession of people. We all walk the same way, stuck within our minds. The anger courses through my body, but I'm raw from the experience of being around others. My mind hangs by the small thread of responsibility to continue living.

Once my face hits the stuffy city air, I inhale the scents of the outdoors: car exhaust, pollution, and the smell of something burning somewhere. I square my shoulders, shove my hands in my pockets and walk towards my house. Having to go to my mother's house weighs on my mind. There is nothing more I want than to live in a world where she doesn't exist.

"Hey, what are you up to for the rest of the day?"

This guy is more persistent than anyone I've ever known before. He isn't the first guy to come around. I've spent most my life fading into the background, becoming invisible. Everything my mother has done over my lifetime has given me the gift of dissociation. Being able to blend into the background is a talent I've mastered.

"What do you want from me?" I turn to face him. Sure he is attractive, but I'm far too emotionally damaged to be loved. Or so I tell myself, because love is a myth to me, proven by the life I've led.

"Just to hang out, I have nothing happening."

I shake my head and, without a second thought, I leave him behind on the sidewalk. I brush my hair away from my face, and the sun's warmth envelops me as I make my way home.

As I open the door, my phone vibrates in my pocket and I answer it quickly. I listen to my mother drone on about her daily life. If only she would stop talking and show some interest in how I'm feeling. To be seen, what would I have to sacrifice? What would I have to do to have her say she's sorry, that she feels bad about the damage she's done?

"You just wouldn't understand. It's adult stuff. Have you been taking care of your apartment or are you going to need help yet again?" her dismissive tone hurts. She's only had to help me one time, but her haranguing is never ending and the more information I give, the more ammo she has.

"Yes. It's done," I say as I take a seat in my apartment. It's a bachelor pad. From the corner chair by the patio window, I can see the layout in its entirety. The smooth tile floor stretches from the kitchen counter to the bathroom door. Despite being a young adult, she still sees me as incapable.

"Best keep it that way. You know how much stress you put on me all the time."

Biting the inside of my lip, I wait for the next assault of words. "I just wish you could be more like other people your age. Just because you are sad doesn't mean you can't go out and make friends. You're wasting your best years, and you'll be devastated when you reach my age and realize all you ever did was give birth to one ungrateful child."

"I have two siblings. What about Michael and Ashley?"

"I said one ungrateful child. You never listen when I talk." She hangs up.

I wonder how many days I'll have to endure the silent treatment.

The days of the past linger over my eyes, when I would plead for her to talk to me, to say anything. Her second favourite weapon of choice is ignoring me, making me gauge her mood to stay safe. I grab my smokes and walk outside. Curling up on the back porch chair, I light a cigarette and watch the smoke twirl away into the air.

Two

Sebastian

It is surprising to see someone so vigilant be so clueless. Despite being completely engrossed in her surroundings, she remains oblivious to my presence. Weeks have passed since dancing the same old dance with her. I'm getting closer every single day. Today, I finally surrendered and let her know of my existence, succumbing to the desire to be seen by my beautiful dove. Her presence brings me peace, a chance to do better, a new opportunity.

My sweet Marla, the woman I've been watching for just over eight months.

Every day I've watched her, and I've never felt the need to speak. The torment behind her eyes draws me to her. Something about her makes me feel. Numbness fades when I watch her, the murderous desires I have inside are quiet for her.

I follow her to the small apartment building, and take up my normal space outside her side window. "Clancy Courts" makes it sound fancier than it is. The six apartments are basic at best. From what I know, her building is clean. It's not a roach hotel. Sometimes I have to come in to clean it for her, but it's the least I can do. She gives me so much already and doesn't even know it. She's on the phone, her dark hair lays across her shoulder, showing me the column of her neck. Her bangs hang in her face, her red lips pressed in a frown. The moment I saw her, I knew I wanted to keep her, *and needed* to keep her as my own.

The allure of my sweet Marla is something that will cut open my chest, pull out my heart and make me beg for the emptiness I've always felt after she breaks me, but I'm willing to risk it all for her. I watch as she walks to the porch, see the flick of the lighter and smell the freshly lit cigarette. She is within arm's reach, but I know it isn't the right time to make my move. My goal is to make her want me above all else, but before that can happen, I need to break her resolve and persuade her to let me in. If all else fails, I'll take her, but for now I'll wait for her to come to me. She's like a caged animal, scared of everyone, of every intention and every word spewed. But I will have her. I'll show her she doesn't need to be afraid anymore.

I walk through the streets. The career path of a drug dealer was never a dream of mine, it was something that fell into my lap and I've been doing the same old actions as if on autopilot mode. Each deal made is another high for them and a low for me. I've been practicing on them, releasing them from their own personal demons, but the time in jail has made me paranoid. It's easy to go for a bid of under two years, but the moment they find out that I snuff the light from people's eyes just because I like to, they'll lock me up and throw away the key.

The night passes me by. Everyone's happy. I get to my supplier's door and have to hand over the money, taking more product. I look into his glassy eyes. He's higher than his clients. As I walk away from his apartment, I ignore the hallways lined with grime, yellowing walls and a staircase that creaks more than it should. Glassy-eyed souls sit at the entrance of the building, and the outdoors are covered in people attempting to get higher than the clouds in the sky.

I get into my car and drive home to the two-story structure. *'A house is not a home without a family.'* The cross stitch in the living room pisses me off. My father should have thought about that before he gave me that last belt lashing. Now the house is just a house, a structure filled with memories that hurt, an empty space filled with too many ghosts. I grab a smoke and light it up, walking out the backdoor to the shed. I turn on the lights, inhaling the musty scent. As I pass the crumbling brick wall, the vibration of my steps causes more of the mortar to break off. It's at least a hundred years old. The house came with a pre-made playpen for bodies. I'll have to spend the next few days digging to make them disappear. Pushing through the plastic panels in the entranceway, I duck through into the larger room, the low ceilings the bane of my existence.

Old pallets and garbage from the past owners lay in the corner. Flicking on the lights, the girl in the metal crate twists and squints. Her eyes are clearer than yesterday, but I know she desires to piss away her life, filling her veins with more drugs than the day before.

"What do you want from me? I don't owe anything," she screams at me.

Money isn't what I want. I want to eradicate the disease from the streets. Taking a long puff, I sit across from her on a wooden chair. "How do you feel?"

"Feel? I feel like fucking shit, you fucking asshole. How the fuck do you think I feel?"

"You stopped puking? Have you learned your lesson?" I ask her, stubbing out my cigarette. I cross the room to stand in front of the metal crate.

"This is to get me clean? You are the fucking asshole who sells the drugs. If you don't want people hooked, maybe don't fucking sell them?"

"Oh, if life was only so easy." I grab the rubber mallet. As soon as I open the door, she breaks into a sprint. The sound of the mallet hitting the back of her head echoes through the room as she hits the floor like a rag doll.

I pick her up from the ground and place her on the table, locking her wrists and ankles with the restraints. Then I hook up the five-gallon bucket to the hoses under the sink of the table. Entering the small room off to the side, I stand surrounded by my tools, picking the ones I want most: pliers and a knife.

Working on her teeth doesn't take long. She doesn't have very many it's a side effect of the poison she chooses to partake. Won't be her problem much longer. Placing them in the container for drying, I take them back to the room. The table is on an angle, propped up on cement blocks so the blood runs towards the sink. I watch her until her eyes flicker open.

"What the fuck?! What the fuck?!" Her lips release a piercing scream as she wrestles against the restraints, her muscles taut and pulsating beneath the skin, but her thin frame is no match for the leather ties I've made. The air reeks of body odour and urine, creating an overpowering stench.

They always say the same things. One time, I'd love for someone to say thank you. Would it be so hard to show some gratitude to the man willing to end your poor excuse of a life?

The knife slides over her jugular, cutting open the skin smoothly. Crimson pours in waves, and I watch as it travels to the head of the table mixing with her stringy hair, and falling through the hoses to the bucket. She grows weaker as her essence leaves her body. The life she led was nothing but a waste, and there's one less soul sucker left in the world.

After washing my tools, I bring them back to the tiny room, untying the long, heavy plastic apron. With a final glance around the musty room, I verify that the stone walls and cement flooring are pristine, exactly as I want them to be. I leave to let gravity do its wonderful magic. Riding my high, I drive around town.

Detouring to Marla's, I watch her sitting in her living room chair, the light reflecting off the blade in her hand. What I wouldn't give to feel her under me, wrap my hands around her throat as she begs for more. Make her really feel truly alive for once.

I watch her slice open the skin on her arm, the beads of blood forming before dripping down her flesh. The relief she must feel, I know that I will do anything to bring her the same euphoria. When her head suddenly turns, I take a step back. After she sets down the blade, she disappears to the bathroom and then lays on her bed.

I wait patiently, I observe until I'm convinced she's drifted off to sleep. As I pull open the window, I listen to the sound of her soft breathing, the only movement being the rise and fall of her chest. I open the closet door near the bathroom and grab some gauze and tape. I sit on the edge of her bed, gazing down at the outline of my perfect dark angel beneath the sheet. Running my thumb over the beads of blood on her skin, I bring it to my lips. The metallic tang of her essence lingers in my mouth, binding me to her. Wanting nothing more than to devour her, bring her to the edge of pleasure and have her moan out my name, I hold myself back. I won't touch her until she wants me just as badly as I desire her. I'm not a complete monster.

Instead, I cover her arm, gently taping the gauze in place. I've been doing little things like this for months, she needs to take better care of herself. Sometimes I bring a small amount of groceries, other times I'm bandaging her. I will do whatever it takes to keep her here with me.

I leave her bedside and pocket the blade before I leave quietly out the window. She must learn that no one can hurt her, and I'll do everything possible to stop her from hurting herself.

Three

Marla

Two days without my mother makes me almost feel like a normal person. The haunting ghost of silent treatment curls around me like a hug from an old friend. I know that no matter how hard I try, she will never love me. There is nothing I can ever do to make her see me or care, and the deafening silence, while lonely, brings me to a place I never knew I needed.

My wish to feel has simmered to a low, dull buzzing in the back of my head, the fresh cut lines on my skin a stinging reminder. I'm unsure where the blade has gone. I've turned my apartment upside down but cannot find it, details blur during a cutting session, and often I don't remember where I've put things. When I'm done here at the centre, I'll go to the hardware store to buy another.

I got here an hour before it opened, hoping to beat the rush and get a number in the mid-fifties. The line is already long and I wonder if an intake will actually help me. Telling someone everything I can within the time restrictions, exposing the family secrets that keep me subdued, quiet, and invisible—would it really fix me? Would I be able to move on with my life? I don't know, but I look around as we enter through the doors. The two older ladies who always come on my day are missing. They remind me of my grandmother before she passed away. Their presence gave me something to look forward to, and now I fear that has been ripped from me.

"Hey, do you know the two ladies that usually sit there?" I ask the man wearing a hat reaching for a number at the same time as me.

"They were chosen yesterday. They went through the back and didn't come out." His mouth forms into a pressed line, not offering any sort of condolences.

I wander to the back, where I always stand, sitting because the news hurts more than I want it to. The rush of emotions covers me. I run my tongue over the inside of my lip to stop the tears. I didn't even know their names. The government decided they weren't worth saving. I fucking hate that they get to choose. Just because they were older doesn't mean that once they were better mentally, they wouldn't contribute to the economy. I loathe that money will always decide someone's worth. The focus should be on people, not the financial benefit.

Hours pass. As the numbers crawl along, emotion bubbles in my chest, and grief runs through me, but I don't want to cry here. Knowing from experience, I cannot cause a scene. Drawing attention to myself is the last thing I want to do, and I've learned that the hard way.

"Hey." His voice again. I glance at him as I swallow the tears. He's wearing dark wash jeans, black boots, a grey band tee, and his hat is backwards.

"Hi."

"How have you been?" he asks. It's the general bullshit question every single person asks you. People's lack of concern for the truth results in them not wanting a real answer. It's just a pleasantry.

"Fine. You?"

"How have you really been?"

Turning to face him, I take in his dark eyes, his narrow nose and the facial hair trimmed along his sharp jawline. He fiddles with his lip ring. His bottom lip is fuller than the top. I wonder what it would be like to kiss him. It's a brief thought. "I've been better. But isn't that right for every single person here?"

"Perhaps some of us don't want to get better, but still do the time." He lowers his hand to my wrist, running his finger over my skin. I stiffen under his touch. "What?"

"Nice bracelets. Do you have a preference or just whatever catches your eye?"

"Just whatever catches my eye. I try to support small businesses when I can. How many tattoos do you have?" I change the subject to him.

"I think almost a hundred. Do you have any?" I shake my head. Making conversation is harder than I thought it would be. His gaze makes me self-conscious and I'm unsure how to react.

"You may like it, it hurts like a bitch for a bit, but then it doesn't and you just vibe to the feeling."

"What's your name?" I dare to ask a question I should have started with.

"Sebastian. What's yours?"

"Marla. Nice to meet you."

"Pleasure is all mine. What number did you get?"

"Fifty-seven. I doubt I'll see the line move enough to get to the intake. What about you?" He holds up a sixty-five and I know he won't get in today.

"Why do they want you here?" I ask.

His tongue skirts out of his mouth to wet his lips. "Anger, apparently. I have issues with it. You?"

"Depression and stuff. Why are you angry?"

He looks away. The swirl of ink on his neck stands out against the dark grey of his shirt. He smells like clean laundry and a masculine citrus cologne. As

I absorb these little details of him, I wonder if my question was too far.

"Not angry, just apparently have a problem with it. Why are you sad and shit?" Smirking, he looks up as the next numbers are called from the P. A. system.

"Just life, trauma and usual shit." The corner of my mouth pulls up into a smile. I'm surprised by the way I feel. The thought of feeling anything from someone else terrifies me as I yearn to make a new connection.

"At this rate, we could just counsel each other and be cured right here in the waiting room," he laughs softly, but it's loud. I dart my eyes around the room to make sure no one is looking.

"They will deem you incurable and end your life. Don't do that."

"Oh, Marla. You care about little ole me?" He looks up at me, a half grin on his lips.

"I don't need to lose more people. Two of the ones I liked disappeared this morning." I close my eyes. He's going to think I'm an idiot. Without waiting for his response, I turn away and twist the bracelet on my wrist. I look towards the large digital number on the wall. Fuck. They are only at twenty-five and it's already almost time to go.

"We're not going to make it today," he says. I don't turn to look at him, knowing he's right, but the tears I've been holding back threaten to slam through my barrier and pour down my face. He keeps talking, offering stupid phrases about how they're in a better place. The pain is over for them. I focus on the chair in front of me. The man sitting there has holes in his jeans. Not the trendy ones, just lived-in holes.

The fake condolences hurt the most, because I don't care if they aren't suffering anymore. What about what I feel? What about what I want? Stopping my thought process, I realize I sound just like my mother. What have I become that I don't care about others? When did I lose all my empathy?

Four

Sebastian

Her mind is spiraling, and I want to stop it before the web she spins is too large. I reach out and grasp her wrist with my hand. Her hazel eyes look into mine. Her bangs need a trim, she's hiding behind her hair again. I saw this happen when I first started watching her. She doesn't stop my touch. I rub my thumb on the underside of her wrist, stroking the soft skin. Her pulse returns to a normal beat. I want to memorize the soft thump, play it in my head to fall asleep or calm me in my own mental storm.

"*Attention, the centre is closing for the day. You can come back tomorrow to get access to the services again*," the lady behind the desk says the words most of us hate hearing. Unlike everyone else, I'm not ordered to be here. I'm here for her.

Marla rips her wrist from my hand and grabs her purse before rushing out the door. By the time I reach the exit, I'm caught up in the mob of people leaving the centre.

I know it'll be almost two days before I see her again. Fucking hell. Glancing behind me, I see her open the door to the hardware store. After giving it a few minutes, I walk into the building. I stay out of view, watching her in an adjacent aisle. It pains me to see her stand in front of the box cutter blade section. On one hand, I'm proud she chooses one of the sharpest blades to slice through her perfect skin, but on the other I hate that she needs this release and that she's marking the skin that belongs to me. I watch as she chooses a three pack. I will have to find them all before taking them away later tonight. Before she's done checking out, I leave the store, walking as slowly as possible.

There is an uncomfortable pause as she looks around and locks eyes with me. "Sebastian. What are you doing here?" She quickly puts her purchase away in her purse

"Was just passing by. Do you want to go for a walk? Coffee? A drink?"

She barely glances at me before looking around. Her eyes fall to the sidewalk. "Um, okay. I could go for a walk."

While we stroll down the sidewalk, I admire her outfit. Her wide-leg pants are cinched at the waist by a metal belt buckle with a delicate pattern. "Where did you find that belt buckle?"

"There's this oddity and retro shop downtown. It's filled with amazing things. Some are pretty far-fetched, but apparently this was worn by Stevie Nicks, which isn't odd or crazy, but I loved the design."

"I'll have to check it out sometime. Is there like skulls and stuff?"

"Yeah, they are far too expensive, as is the jewellery made from bones, teeth, and other retro stuff. One day, maybe."

We walk for a while without a word. The comfort I feel with her calms the angry beast that lies within my mind. I don't think about taking away lives when I'm with her. My focus is on protecting her. We find a bench in the park. The trees have started to bloom, and the grass is still that weird colour before it turns a rich green. I take a seat. We're so close to her home. I want to make sure she is mentally okay from today before she leaves and is alone.

I light a smoke and think about the body to dispose of at home. I would rather spend every waking hour with Marla.

"Can I bum one from you?" I pass her the cigarette from my lips, watching the smoke curl between us. She holds it delicately, her eyes flickering up to meet mine. The sound of the lighter sparking echoes in the silence as I light another and give her a smirk.

"Plans tonight?" I ask. She shakes her head. Her lips leave a red shade on the filter.

She shakes her head and asks, "Do you?" Her lips leave a red shade on the cigarette filter.

I rub my tongue over my lip ring. "Nah, not really." She looks away, takes a few drags before she snubs out the butt.

"What do you do for work?" she asks, her head turned to look at me.

"I'm in sales, you?"

"Freelance stuff. I like it because I don't have to follow a schedule and can do the work when I want." She flips her hair over her shoulder. The scent of vanilla and tobacco lingers in the air. From being in her house, I know the perfume she wears, the air fresheners she uses—everything down to what beauty products she likes.

"Well, this has been fun. I've got to get home, though. I'll see you 'round." She smiles at me before she walks across the street.

I don't leave the bench until she is out of view. As I stroll down the road, the houses loom over me, their windows reflecting the evening light. When I get to the first customer's house, he's already giving me a hard time. "This week's stuff is shit. When are you going to get the good shit?" I sigh, shrug my shoulders, and wait at the door. "Fine, whatever."

He hands me his money and closes the door in my face.

The rest of the night flows similarly. I don't make the shit, I don't even test it. I wouldn't know if it was good or not, because my addiction will never be drugs. I'm consumed with the need for Marla, to reach each high I can with her until the end of our days.

On my drive home, I think about how to help Marla open up more. I'm tired of waiting. Watching her has been my favourite pastime, but now that I've spoken to her, nothing is better. Parking my car in the laneway, I walk inside to change my clothes. I slip on old jeans, a stained t-shirt and grab a drink of water. I push the wheelbarrow from behind the house to the shed, unlocking the door to the wall.

As I stand above the four bodies, the putrid odour of decay fills my nostrils. I've waited too long to dispose of them, maggots have already started. With a swift motion, I grab the guy from under his arms. The weight of his body makes it difficult for me to move him towards the wheelbarrow.

The burial hole was already started. After a couple of hours of digging, I am finally satisfied with the depth. I dump the man's corpse, turn and hold the handles of the wheelbarrow behind me as I walk back to the shed. This time I'm able to fit two bodies into the wheelbarrow and it's about the same weight.

These girls had spitfire, I'll give them that, but they weren't a match against me. They withered away rather quickly. I finish up the last body and take the fresh one off the table. I hoist her over my shoulder, and I put her on the pile.

I spend an hour refilling the hole, thankful I live in the outskirts of town and that many trees cover my property. I head inside to strip out of these clothes and have a shower.

After bathing, I sit at the kitchen table and eat a sandwich. My fingers drum on the table as my thoughts are consumed by Marla.

I want nothing more than to be the spark that puts the fire back in her eyes. I know we are soulmates. She is mine and I'll forever be hers, even if she doesn't know it yet. My jaw clenches thinking of all the time we've wasted already being apart. Without another thought, I leave the house and drive my car back to town. When I look through the window, she's at the door talking to a man.

My stomach churns at the thought of another man touching her. He reaches his hand out to her face, his finger pushing the hair out of her eyes. Her head shakes, she backs up slightly and this fucking scab advances. His eyes flick up to the window. I don't move, but he does. Leaving the door open, he backs out of it to the hall before he's gone. I watch her close and lock the door. She wraps her arms around herself and walks away to her bedroom.

"Who the fuck are you and why the fuck are you watching my tenants?" he yells from behind me.

Turning around, I purse my lips before speaking. "Sorry, sir, I have no idea what you are talking about." I look around at the other buildings and houses, pulling a scrap piece of paper out of my pocket. "This isn't 83 Arbor lane?"

His eyebrows raise, and he takes a step closer. "I know you were fucking watching her. I'll call the police."

"What's going on?" My sweet Marla stands on the sidewalk, her arms across her stomach, holding her sides. I swing my gaze to the landlord, cocking an eyebrow. He says nothing.

"Hey Marla, sorry I was looking for an address and think I got lost. This guy started yelling and then you came out."

His face turns red. "That isn't it at all, Marla. This guy was peeping in your windows, and I came out to take care of it. Run along inside and let a man take care of this." Anger flashes through her eyes, she unfolds her arms as she looks from him to me. "Sebastian?"

"I know how this must look. I'm out on a service call and got turned around is all. I'm sorry to ruin your night. I had no idea where you lived." Shoving the piece of paper back in my pocket, I clench my jaw and turn away.

"Peter, this is my friend Sebastian." Her voice is music to my ears, "Sebastian, this is my landlord who was just leaving." I turn to face both of them, a strained smile on my face when I look towards him.

"Marla, I'll talk to you later," her landlord spits out before walking away.

I turn to her and rest my hand on her shoulder, noticing she doesn't move. "Are you okay?" I ask, staring down into her eyes.

"Yeah, he's just a creep. Have a good night, Sebastian." She touches my arm before she walks away.

Glancing at my wrist, I check the time on my watch. I'll have to risk running late tonight. As I rush to my car, I can feel my heart pounding in my chest, but once I drive slowly, I feel more relaxed. I see the landlord getting into a van and follow him to an office. I grab a rubber mallet from the backseat and walk towards him before he enters.

"Jesus! Fuck. What the hell, man?" He spins on his heels to look at me. "You scared the shit out of me, you fucking psychopath." His reaction causes an involuntary grin and without waiting another minute, I strike him with the mallet and watch as he falls to my feet.

Five

Marla

What a weird night it has been so far. Peter came around to talk about fixing my tap in the kitchen, but as per usual, was a gross pig. The smell of sweat and rotten eggs emanated from him, and just like in the past, he tried to touch me. I shudder at the thought. Last year, he was under the premise of fixing something in my bathroom and instead all my drawers were open when I returned. Closing the door, I think it's over until I hear voices yelling outside. As I run out to the front sidewalk, I see Sebastian facing me, standing in front of Peter, who looks over his shoulder at me.

Sebastian's dark brown eyes stare into my soul. He sees me in a way that I feel like I matter. It's dangerous, feeling that way, like another person could accept you for who you are. Every broken piece, every scar, and the demons within. After listening to them talk and explain, I really think Peter is just an asshole and Sebastian got lost trying to do his job.

After I head back inside, I walk to my bedroom to unwrap the blades from the package, three this time, I shouldn't lose them again. The pain inside rolls through me. Every emotion I can't name pokes at the surface for me to acknowledge it is there. I want nothing more than to silence every feeling. There is no middle ground though. Either I feel everything at a magnitude that I can't stomach, or I feel nothing at all. That is why Sebastian scares me, because his presence lately has calmed the emotions and sparked something deep inside. I sit on the edge of my bed and hold the blade. My phone rings before I can make the first cut. Sighing, I lay down the sharp box cutter and walk to my phone. I guess mother has stopped the silent treatment.

"Hello," I say as I walk to the kitchen to pour cold coffee into a mug.

"Hello? Hello? That's all you have to say to me? You haven't called in days, not even a message or anything. How dare you?" Her voice pricks me like a rose thorn, I want to cut her off when she acts this way.

"I'm sorry. I thought you wanted your space," I mutter, taking a sip of the old coffee, bitter and cold.

"You are being silly. I love you. Have you been working at least?" Her words still have the power to hurt me. At least twenty years of this, and I can already feel the tears welling up inside. I can't cut her off, all I want is for her to love me.

"Yes. I'm sorry, mom. I thought you wanted space. You were mad the last time we talked."

"I wasn't mad. I was disappointed. There is a difference. I've been fine, thanks for asking. I want you to come over tomorrow night. I'll make dinner. We'll have fun, I promise." Fear fills me. I know fun will never happen.

"I'll be there. How are you?"

"Five, be here at five." With that, she hangs up. Never feeling good enough for her is something I should be used to. She has spent my entire life making sure I know that I'm worth nothing. Every word, every step of neglect, every lie has been another piece added to the pile to show me I'm worth nothing to her.

Walking back to my bedroom, I shrug out of my sweater and pick up the blade and hold it to my skin. As I watch the beads of blood bubble out of the cut, bliss hits me first. Making a second cut under the first, I watch the lines of blood drip together against the scar tissue of the past and I'm able to breathe.

I slide the blade across the skin for the third time. The emotions are silent and the room spins slightly.

I close my eyes and I revel in the feeling. If only I could feel this free all the time. Except I know better than anyone that I will never reach the first time again. The first time I ever cut myself was by far the best and I'll probably spend my life chasing it.

After sitting in the same spot for a while, I get up and go to the bathroom. I wash my arm, cover it with antiseptic cream and change into a tank and sleep shorts. Then I slip into my bed and fall asleep.

I wake to darkness, the shadows from the streetlights dancing across the walls. A creaking sound fills my apartment and I scramble out of bed. Walking to the living room, I note nothing is out of place. The lock is still latched on the door, and everything is silent. I try to recall the dream I was having. The last dregs linger, but not enough for me to grab onto the last piece. As I look at my arm, I realize it's wrapped in a bandage, and a faint smell of antiseptic fills my nostrils.

Padding over to my favourite chair, and sitting down I don't remember putting on a bandage, but details usually get fuzzy after I self-harm. I settle into a comfortable position, pulling my legs under me, and grab a soft throw pillow. I place it under my head. Darkness grasps me and pulls me under quickly.

The day passes rapidly, working on a lot of the projects that I haven't had the mental capacity to get done. Hitting the send button on a completed project is my favourite part. The thrill of doing something right is needed lately for the validation it gives me. I finish as much as I can, before four PM. I'm able to clear my calendar for the week and it gives me hope that I will pick up some extra jobs. Working from home can be a very isolating thing, but it also gives me the opportunity to not have to face people. It can be a double-edged sword in a lot of ways. I turn off my computer and walk to the bathroom.

I brush my hair, trying different styles so my mother doesn't notice that I haven't had the ability to get a haircut. Finally, I just tie it up into a high ponytail and style the bangs in a side sweep. Picking up my phone, I order an Uber before walking to my bedroom. I pull on a black sweater and pair it with burgundy jeans.

On the way to my mother's house, I consider how to address her. I would like her to stop treating me like I'm a child. It's been five years of me living on my own, and I'm ready for her to see me as the adult I have grown into. Lost in my thoughts, I bite the inside of my lip absentmindedly. My concern is that either way my actions will have negative consequences, and she'll blow them out of proportion.

As the Uber pulls into the driveway, I see only my mother's car. I give the driver a five-dollar bill. "Would you be able to pick me up again? I liked the service you gave." He nods, and shows me on my phone how I can request certain drivers. I like that he didn't talk.

The large wooden house stands in front of me. Taking a deep breath, I brace myself as I walk to the door and ring the bell. A few minutes pass before she appears at the window in the door. Her pin-straight, dark brown hair is freshly coloured. Her green eyes look at me over her square glasses, her face perfectly made up. Mother opens the door, her cold eyes judging me like they always do. The tension in my jaw increases, and I want to flee, but I stand as tall as I can.

"Glad you could make it on time. How are you?" Her smile is wide, but doesn't reach her eyes. Most of the time, I feel like we're puppets in a play. She acts for a camera that doesn't exist and I do my best to blend in and play the way she wants me to.

"Hey, mom. How are you?" Entering the house of memories, the walls lined with every single lie, every ghost of the past. I follow her up the stairs, glancing down toward the basement, but the door is closed. My brother used to live down in the basement but recently moved out. He is the star child, the one who can do no wrong. Almost as toxic as my mother, even though I'm the oldest. My sister lives around the corner and seems to escape most of mother's wrath, but is just like my mom. My sister acts for the camera of life, she dreams of the fans she doesn't really have and I don't know why I'm different.

"I've been cooking all day. I hope that you still eat turkey."

Walking into the kitchen, the clutter surrounds me. China cabinets filled to the brim with knick-knacks, old pictures, and newspapers stacked high. The house is a contradiction. The outside looks perfectly on display, while the inside is home to more junk than anyone would need in their lifetime.

"Did you cook an entire Thanksgiving dinner?" I look at the bowls of mashed potatoes, green bean casserole, corn, and a plate of turkey that line the white counter.

"You could just be appreciative. Grab a plate."

I open the cupboard and pull out a plate, then add mashed potatoes, corn, a tiny amount of green bean casserole and a slice of turkey to it. She shakes her head and glances from my plate to the spread of food. "I guess you can always get seconds," she says as she fills her plate. We walk around the corner of the kitchen to the dining room.

"What's new and exciting?" she asks me, and I ponder the question. She's in a good mood and I allow myself to believe that this is just about dinner.

"I've had a bunch of freelance projects and they have been going really well. One of my clients wants to hire me full-time."

"Did you hear from your sister? She made manager at her job. We're just so proud of her." She smiles as she scoops mashed potatoes into her mouth. If only I could matter to her as much as everyone else does.

"I haven't talked to her yet. Good for her, she's been working hard." I reach for the water and pour it into the glass next to my plate.

"Be careful. You don't want to break that pitcher. It's been in the family for years." My hand shakes as the confrontation I know is going to happen runs through my body. I take a sip of water and eat a few forkfuls of green bean casserole.

"Mom, I want to talk to you about treating me like an adult. I don't like it when you treat me like a child. I'm twenty-five and I've been living alone successfully for over five years." I look into her eyes. A darkness passes through them before her face softens.

"Marla, I wouldn't have to treat you that way if you just took care of yourself. Look at your brother.

He's doing a great job at growing into a respectful adult."

Cutting into my turkey, I take a bite before I talk again, the haunting whispers telling me to keep the peace floss through my mind. "I just think, after everything we've been through, that you could do this for me."

She rolls her eyes, and sets down her fork. "I know that it's hard for you since your father died, but he wasn't just your dad, he was someone I loved deeply and now it's up to me to take care of you."

I set down the fork and knife, keeping them in my hands, the cool metal digging into my palms from holding on so tightly. "Dad doesn't have anything to do with what I'm talking about. I want you to stop treating me like a child. I've been through enough, and I need you to treat me like the adult I've be-come."

She laughs, the joke is lost on me. "Been through a lot, have you? Because I didn't praise you enough growing up, or is it because you are jealous of your brother and sister, and you want to paint me as a terrible mother?" I take my phone from my pocket and order myself an Uber. I can't stay here another moment, the vice on my chest tightens with each breath I take and my heart thumps quicker than it should.

"Are you leaving? You can't just walk away. We're in the middle of dinner."

"I'm full. It's been lovely, but I have to leave." The tears build in my chest. She can never love me.

"Marla, sit down right now. You are being so dramatic. What has gotten into you? You have always been the quiet one. Like a shy dog that hangs in the background, that is who you are."

"Goodbye mom, I'll call you soon. Love you."

She grabs my arm before I can leave the kitchen. She spins me towards her, and her palm connects with my cheek. The pain spreads across my face, the tears threaten to fall and my phone pings with an alert that the Uber is here. "You are an ungrateful little cunt." I stare into her green eyes, and it's almost as if I can see the mask slip back into place. "I'll call you soon. Have a good night," the words drip off her tongue like venom. I know that this will grant me either days of the silent treatment or endless calls.

I grab my purse and run down the stairs. Once I'm outside in the cool air, I'm able to breathe again. I get into the back of the Uber and ride home in silence. If only there was a way to quiet my mind. The memories slaughter me, breaking what's left of my heart, and eat away at my soul.

Back inside my apartment, I lock the door and my knees go weak as I walk to the patio. I sit in the chair and light a cigarette, exhaling as the tears start to pour. I do nothing to stop them as the sobs wrack my body.

Sebastian

The last few days have been busy. The uptick in business has been great, but I've been missing Marla and being away from her fuels the fury I carry deep in the pit of my stomach. Taking Peter the other night was a physical feat. The guy must weigh at least two hundred pounds and my muscles still ache from dragging him.

Securing him in the cage was easy, but all he does is yell. Giving him water and food once a day doesn't seem to quiet him. Last night when I went to my supplier Clyde's house to exchange money for goods, he was high as a kite and pushed a short blonde woman out the door towards me. How un-expected that she all but landed in my lap. I took her home, and that was the straightforward part. The promise of drugs was too tempting. She was like a moth to a flame, not realizing she was going to be burned in the shed. She's working off the high in the crate next to Peter.

I've spent the day in the garden. At first glance, you wouldn't peg me for a gardening aficionado but that's the problem with first impressions. My dove sees me under everything, that's why I need to have her. Still fixing the damage that happened to my flowers while I was in prison last time frustrates me. The hydrangeas are my favourite flower. The large purple bursts of colour mix nicely with the pink and white ones. The nitrogen and phosphates from the blood–the essence of somebody–makes them bloom so beautifully, creating an oasis of colour behind the house. Lilies, ferns, and hostas separate the arrangement with the earth's green colour of life.

I drive to the mental health centre and look through the herd of people, but she isn't there. The next place I go is to her house. I don't see her at her desk, and I don't want to risk getting caught. Since the day I first spoke to her, her voice curbs the anger inside. That isn't something I'm willing to give up anytime soon. I need her, but I'll be back after I take care of some pressing matters. I drive home and open Peter's crate. "What the fuck do you want from me?" He paces, his eyes flick from me to the entranceway. I'm sure he thinks he has a chance to escape.

"I want your building." I don't take my eyes off of him.

"If I let you have the building, you'll let me go?" I give him a half smile and put my hands up. "I knew you were looking at that freak, Marla. She won't bend for you. She doesn't bend for anyone," his words grate my nerves. I want to see what makes him tick, how much pain he can endure. He doesn't deserve her, of course she wouldn't bend for him. He's the scum of the earth, a virus that needs to be eradicated. My focus is shattered as screams surround us. The new girl is awake.

"My name is SYLVIE and I refuse to die." The screams make Peter jump and I use the time he's distracted to latch his wrist with a restraint. With him attached to the wall, I open her crate and pull her across the cement.

"Fuck you, you sick fucker." Her nails dig into my arm, and I drop her. Sylvie's knees skin against the floor and she takes one glance back at me as she runs. She doesn't get far as her body gets caught in the wide plastic panels. It looks easy to run through, but they wrap around your body like they have a mind of their own.

With a firm grasp on her ponytail, I yank her across the floor and seize her wrist in the restraint. As they both come to terms with being tied like animals, I clean the floor. The sight of skin and blood give me a wave of disgust. It's appalling how repulsive humans can be.

"What do you want?" she screams.

"Touch her." I back up to stand across from them, leaning on the tool bench and crossing my ankles.

"What the fuck? I'm not doing that. What the fuck is wrong with you?" Peter shouts.

The woman starts to cry and scream. "My name is Sylvie, and I don't want to die here. You are a fucking sicko."

I smile, wondering if she thinks repeating her name is going to make me stop. That bringing humanity into the equation is going to make me falter. I scoff, I lost my humanity a long time ago. "Obviously."

Peter spits on the floor, his face red, and he struggles against the restraint. "I won't do it. Fuck you."

I lean down towards them. "Listen, the last person you touch before you die will not be my Marla. I don't give a fuck if you want to hit or rape Sylvie, but you will fucking touch her."

A large puddle of piss forms beneath the both of them, and I crinkle my nose at the smell. Taking a step forward, I inspect both restraints carefully. Once I'm satisfied they are secure, I walk away. "Enjoy. I'll be back later to take care of you."

Locking the shed door from the outside, I walk into the house to change my clothes. I grab a sandwich and walk out to the car, then drive to town. After my sales are complete, I stroll to Marla's apartment.

She sits up in her favourite chair, her face tear stained. It breaks my heart and I want to know who has hurt her. My eyes wander to the blade that sits on the coffee table. I wish I could suck the blackness that clouds her mind out of her. I'd take everything on as my own if it meant that she could live a life of freedom. I'll slay every demon that takes up real estate in her head.

My phone buzzes, lit with Clyde's number. Walking away from the window, I make my way to his apartment to exchange money for his product, and then I make my way back to my car. I'll finish up everything tonight and tomorrow I'll find out what is wrong. I don't want to take her against her will, but if it means keeping her safe, I will do whatever it takes.

When I get to the shed, the lock is still secured. Opening it, I make my way through to the final room to see Sylvie on the floor without her shorts on. She's curled in a ball crying and Peter is looking away with his pants open, his limp dick laying exposed against his underwear.

"Well, well. I knew you were a sick fuck, but I really didn't see this happening. Any hole is better than no hole before death, I guess." I put on my apron and cross the room, unlatching Sylvie. I pick her up and cradle her in my arms.

"Why did you let that monster do that?" She sniffles, her face a mess of tears and snot.

"It's just the way it had to be. He was in control and did this to you. Not me."

I lay her on the table, securing her wrists and ankles. "I don't want to die," she whispers, sniffling the snot back into her nose.

"Your death is for a reason. Your essence will grow the biggest and most beautiful flowers." Her eyes follow me as I open the door to the small room, grabbing the pliers and a knife.

"What do you mean?" Her voice trembles and I tilt my head to look down at her, deciding I will wait to extract her teeth. She's been through a lot. I must be going soft.

Peter stares at us across the room and if I had the right restraints, I'd pull him over to watch. Hooking up the hose to the bucket and the table, I slide the knife swiftly over her jugular and watch the life leave her eyes slowly. A peaceful look falls over her features, something she didn't experience in life and I provided this gift.

"You are a lowlife human. Marla will want nothing to do with you." His words creep through my mind. They bounce between the demons that live inside my head. He is telling me words I never want to hear, but I know aren't true. She will love me in her own time.

I walk over to him, my footsteps echoing off the walls, and I lean down to hold the pliers to his hand. Tonight will be the exception to my rules, I'll make the floor red with his blood. The sound of ripping flesh echoes as I forcefully pull off the first fingernail. I try my best to ignore his screams as I finish up. The palpable fear in the air gives me a rush of euphoria. Everything within me quiets, and I work on the rest of his nails.

"She already loves me. She just doesn't know it yet," I whisper as he grunts under the pain. I walk over to the table, disconnect the tubes, and move the bucket over to the side where it can't fall over. Using the same pliers, I use one hand to hold her mouth open and pull out each tooth with the other.

Entering the small room, I put her teeth in a dish with rubbing alcohol and pour some onto Peter's hands. As I move to the table to pick up Sylvie, he screams out about what an asshole I am. Dark laughter erupts from my chest, as I hoist her over my shoulder. I walk with Sylvie to the brick enclosed room, the place where I keep all the bodies until

I'm ready to bury them, covering her with a mixture of lime and lye.

"What are you going to do, tough guy? Haul me up onto the table and drain me of blood? Are you some sort of vampire freak?" He peppers me with questions. I stand in front of him and think about how I want to kill him.

"Blood is rich in phosphorous, potassium and nitrogen, which is really great for plant growth. My garden grows better than anyone else's."

"You are a freak. Marla will never love you. I've been her landlord for two years, and I know her more than you ever will."

Launching toward him, I viciously grip his chin with my hand. The fury rolls through me, the words on my lips stop before they can come out. "You aren't worth my breath, and you are too dense to understand our love."

I get up and walk to the small room and pick up my saw, put back the pliers, and grab the knife. As I stalk back toward him, I slide the knife across his face. Once for the disrespect he's shown me, and twice for the complications he has added to my life. I continue cutting him for the disrespect of Marla until his face is in tattered ribbons. His flesh hangs loosely from the sides of his head, the muscles stare back at me.

"Is that the best you got?" he croaks out. I trail the knife down what's left of his chin, wanting to cut out his vocal cords, but wanting to prolong his suffering for daring to touch my woman.

When I start the power saw, his eyes bulge and urine soaks his grimy pants. I lower the blade to his shoulder, cutting through the muscles and tendons as I push harder to get through the bone. Vibrations of the saw run through my arms, and blood and bone spray around. I finish the other arm and when I turn off the blade I stare at my beautiful work. Once I'm done, I drag the pieces of his body to the concrete formation by the stairs. "Fuck you both. Rot in hell."

As I mop up the blood, using hydrogen peroxide and going over it with water, I listen to music. Each song relates back to Marla in some way. She consumes everything I do. After the tools are clean and the floors are better than they were, I sprinkle powder to soak up the urine and blood. Since it's past midnight, I lock up and stroll into the house.

I get into the shower, the comforting heat of the water beads against my skin, washing the blood from my skin and scrubbing the pieces of flesh and bone out of my hair. As I enter my bedroom, I look over my fake social media accounts to see if she's posted anything, but there is nothing. She doesn't post often, but when she does, it means everything to me. I miss her. I need her as much as someone needs their next high.

Seven

Marla

When I collect my number, a letter is placed in my hand. I'm preparing myself for my first fine, money is always an issue and I worry further. As I open the envelope, a thin piece of paper flutters to the ground. A hundred dollars is the consequence of missing an appointed day. I clutch the paper tightly as I make my way to the back of the room. A sense of unease washes over me as I take in all the unfamiliar faces today, my mind wandering to the ones who were here with me on the last day.

I push the letter into my purse, and a quick check of my phone shows many texts from Mother. She's in the love bombing stage, the point in time where she pretends to love me so I'll come crawling back. I know I will, but this time stings, not because of the words or her hands on my skin but because all I did was ask to be treated like the adult I am.

When I swallow the lump in my throat, the tears fight their way to the surface, and I slump down on the floor, lean my back against the wall, and tilt my face to the ceiling. I close my eyes and try to push away the overwhelming sadness that threatens to make me cry. No matter how hard she tries, mother won't ever fully break me today. I'll hold back my tears and keep my dignity in public.

The scent of his laundry soap fills my nostrils, I smell him before I see him. His shoulder pushes against mine as he sits beside me. "Missed you the other day. Where were you?"

I glance over, and take in his tattooed hands, fingers bouncing on his jean-clad knees. My gaze travels up towards his face, his dark hair is parted on the side but still messy, his tongue runs over his lip, and his dark brown eyes have thick lashes that I hadn't noticed before. "Things came up." I turn my head to look away.

Sebastian's fingers shoot out and grasp my jaw, turning my chin to look at him. His sudden touch is like fire. I can't remember the last time someone touched me and I felt something.

"What things?" His eyes stare deep into mine like he can see my dark, twisted soul and he isn't scared.

"Shitty things. Don't worry, I got my fine."

His fingers linger for a moment longer before dropping. "I'm not worried about your fine. I'm worried about you," his whisper brings me comfort. I've only ever wanted someone to give a shit about me.

"Do you want to go for a walk after this?" he asks. I stare straight ahead, and the emotional turmoil rolls over my body. I desire to know this guy, but what will it cost him? What's the point in anything if I'll never get the help?

"Wasn't a marriage proposal. We'll save that for at least the fifth date." When I look in his direction, his tongue is in his cheek and his eyebrows are raised.

"Deal. No marriage until at least the fifth date." My lips curve into a smile I can't hold back.

"Nah, I said a proposal by the fifth date. Marriage? Phew, that's gotta be like eighth date stuff."

I shake my head, and my chest shakes from the struggle to keep the laugh deep inside. Sebastian is a breath of fresh air. It's like I've been drowning my entire life, and he's come into my world to give me the air to breathe again.

The announcement comes over the loudspeaker like it does every single time I'm here. I glance down at my number and see I was only five away from being able to have an intake. I walk to the desk and swipe my debit card for the fine, the progress I've made saving money sliced in half.

"Where do you want to walk to?" Sebastian asks as we walk out the door. I shrug my shoulders. Never having gone anywhere here in town, I wouldn't know where to start.

"Wherever is fine."

He directs me around the corner from the building. "So, ready to tell me what kept you away from here? I'm sure it wasn't that you wanted to donate to the charity."

The corner of my mouth turns up, and the rest of my face stays in resting bitch face mode. "The saddest thing about me is that I was born to someone who could never love me. She's never cared enough to try, and the only comfort she brings is pain."

He's silent for a while, and we continue to walk. "The only sad part is that she really misses out on being with a wonderful person like you. Fuck her."

"It would make sense if I wasn't so unlovable. She can love my siblings. She's been the catalyst for everything that has happened to me, which makes me feel like a horrible person because I'm probably going to end up just like her if I blame her for my trauma. And at the end of the day, I just want her to tell me she loves me and mean it." Oh good, I've trauma-dumped on the first person to show me any attention in years.

"You aren't a horrible person. When my dad used to beat me with different tools, I didn't become him when I grew up angry. When my mother took off when I was little, it didn't make me unlovable because she couldn't stand up to the job. I'd never end up like them, nor will you end up like her. It's her loss if she can't see that there are so many reasons to love you."

His honesty makes me feel less alone, like I didn't just dump half my life story on him. We connect in a way. As we continue walking, his fingers lace with mine. I don't pull away, and we soon arrive near my apartment. "I'm sorry, I shouldn't trauma-dump on you. It's not a competition." We walk to my apartment, and his gaze slides over to me as we continue at a slow pace.

"It's not a competition we'll ever win. Every piece of trauma is a shattered piece of memory holding us together in the only way we know how. Trauma becomes a comfort blanket that wraps us in the darkest hug. The experiences that formed us, that changed our brain chemistry, are all our own. No one can ever feel the pain we feel, because every fractured piece is only our own." His words sink in. I've never heard someone explain it that way.

"You are right, it doesn't make it hurt less, but it makes things clearer." When we reach my door, I don't know what to do. My eyes dart around, and I wring my hands together, I couldn't be more socially awkward if I tried.

"I don't have to work tonight. Do you want to order dinner?" he asks me.

I nod. "Yeah, actually, that sounds really nice." I unlock the door, and we walk inside. "My apartment isn't anything special, but it's mine," I say after we do a small circle around the tiny place.

"It's you, and that's all that matters."

After I walk to the kitchen to make us tea, I look over my shoulder, "Whatever you want to order is good with me. I'm pretty easy," I say as his eyes burn into mine. Sitting on the chair in my living room, he looks like he's always been here. It's unsettling and comforting all at once. Everything about his appearance is everything my mother would hate.

"What's your favourite meal in the world?" he asks as I bring the tea to the living room. I've never really thought about it. I wasn't allowed to have a favourite anything growing up, and I wonder if that's what doesn't make me qualified to be an adult now. "It's a simple question. I didn't ask you if you're ready to move in together."

I bite the inside of my lip to stop from laughing. "Nah, that's definitely third date shit." His grin stretches across his face, and the light glints off the silver ring piercing in his lip.

"Um, tacos?"

"Are you asking me if you like tacos? Or are you shouting that you, in fact, want tacos to be your favourite food?" His eyebrow arches and a coy smile crosses over his lips.

"I want tacos to be my favourite." I beam, and he laughs. While I pull out my phone to order, he drinks his tea. "What do you want?"

"Whatever you get, I'll get. It's my treat today. I'm not the one with the fine." I almost roll my eyes. I'd already paid it, but I appreciate his offer. "Did your mother not allow you to have any favourites? Or did she just make you feel like you didn't deserve to have any?"

Tucking my hair behind my ear, I roll the question over in my mind. "The latter, I guess. I believed, since no one cared about me, it didn't matter what I liked. My grandparents were the best thing to ever happen to me, but they lived far away and only came over occasionally. We used to watch British comedies and stay up past my bedtime." The memory washes over me. My heart aches for the time I had with them.

"We could probably stream some reruns with tacos. Sounds like a good time to me."

I smile, the ache inside replaced with a warm sensation. He picks up the remote for the television and fiddles around with it until the internet loads on the screen. "Do you recall the name of the show?" I shake my head, trying my best to wrack my brain and memories, but I don't remember.

There is a loud knock at the door. "It's all good. I'll look and see who is here." He hands me the remote and walks to the front door. I scroll through the choices. When I find the one I want, he is back with the tacos.

"It's a nice building. How long have you lived here?" he asks, splitting up the food and handing me the container.

"Five years. You don't have to lie, it's a shithole. But it's affordable, and although the landlord is a creep, the other neighbours are good." He only nods as he digs into his food. We watch television until we're done eating. He grabs the garbage from dinner and walks to the kitchen.

"Is this your patio?" His head tilts to the glass doors.

"Yeah, the garbage is out there. I'll join you."

Walking to the kitchen, I grab my smokes and a lighter, and we go outside to sit on the white plastic chairs. He throws the garbage in the can, and we look over the back road. "Beautiful view, eh?" His laugh makes me smile.

"Could always be worse, like having to look into the house behind you. When I was growing up, one place I lived with my dad had that. We'd look out the kitchen window, and you'd be looking into the kitchen of your neighbour. Many people don't like blinds, apparently." This time, I do laugh.

When we finish smoking, I walk him to the door to leave. "I'll see you soon, eh?" Sebastian says as his hands brace the door frame. My eyes scan over his body until I focus on his lips, the way his tongue plays over his piercing makes me wish he was play-ing with me.

"Yeah, soon," I whisper. His eyes focus on mine as he leans into the doorway and presses a kiss on my forehead. He's gone before I can process it, as much as I want his lips on mine, the battle within my head is too much to pursue.

As the weeks pass, my routine settles into a pattern of mental health clinic visits, striving for excellence at work, and enjoyable walks with Sebastian. Our conversations have become the highlight of my day, and I look forward to them. Each day is slightly better.

I've talked to my mother. She has apologized at least a hundred times, and although I know things won't actually improve, I let it slide for now. I've only taken one night with the blade against my skin to mark it. When Sebastian disappears, I fear I won't have control over how many slices I make. Holding onto my reservation so tightly has hurt my mind. The thoughts swirl too much and I realize I have to let go at least a little. He has shown me nothing but kindness, and not everyone is going to be like my family. Not everyone wants to hurt me on purpose.

Eight

Sebastian

Over the last couple weeks of hanging out, the carefree side of her that I get to see up close versus in the shadows makes me almost giddy. My love makes her feel lighter, just like I hoped it would. I wonder if my love can clear the dark from her mind and give her the life she deserves. We're sitting on her porch. There isn't a cloud in the sky, and although the sun shines down, the breeze brings a coldness in the air.

"Do you think we'll ever get an intake number?" she asks me, her smile gone, and I know that I'll have to figure out how to fix her.

"I'm not sure. Sometimes, I think that the darkness that surrounds me adds character."

"Bullshit, that's just what you tell yourself to feel better," she says. Her hazel eyes dance over my face.

"Yeah, maybe, but it works. Feed the masses the fine answer, and no one will bat an eye," I say, but she doesn't respond. She takes the final drag off her cigarette and stubs it into the ashtray that sits on a milk crate. "Fancy furniture out here, I see." Stubbing out my own, I look at her.

"I'm sure your house is so much better." Her bangs fall in her face again, and she moves them.

"Nah, I got my dad's house, retro furniture and all. Are you growing your bangs out?" She stands from the chair and disappears inside without answering my question. I follow her.

"I'm sorry, Marla, if I'm out of line, you can tell me I'm an asshole." I'm worried I've overstepped. Her warm hand in mine, and countless words exchanged make me not want to go back to just watching her.

"I have trouble finding a hairdresser. It's stupid. I'm just bad at taking care of myself." I look down into her eyes before she glances away.

"Don't do that, self-care is hard when you are depressed. Hell even when you're not, it's hard. Can I cut your hair?"

She tilts her head up to look at me. "Okay."

"I cut my hair. I don't know if that is reassuring or devastating to hear, but I'd love to take the pressure off your mind and help you out." Her eyes soften, and her red lips curve into a smile. I lean against the counter as she disappears into the bathroom. Opening the patio door, I grab one of the plastic chairs and put it in the kitchen as she returns with supplies.

"Sebastian's Hair Salon is open." I point to the chair, and she shakes her head and hands me a pair of scissors and a brush. She holds a towel around her shoulders. "Just a trim? and tidy up the bangs?" I hope so. Her hair suits her face so perfectly.

"Yeah, that is perfect." I brush out her hair slowly, enjoying the wafting smell of her shampoo scent, jasmine, and something I can't place. The silence that covers us is welcome and comforting. I work slowly through cutting her hair and move to the front to work on her bangs. "Check in the mirror before you kill me." I grin a crooked smile.

While she goes to check her hair, I see a broom and dustpan next to her fridge and clean up the floor.

"I love it. Thank you so much," she says as she walks into the room. I turn to look at her beauty, and my breath catches in my throat. She stalks toward me and throws her arms around my neck, stretching on her tippy toes until her lips find mine. My hands go to her lower back, and I hold her against me. Feeling her fingertips run over the back of my neck sends shivers throughout my body. I deepen the kiss, and she doesn't back away. Her body against mine is like the puzzle piece I've been missing. I know that I've made the right choice in her, all the months of watching. Every moment sacrificed for her has led me here.

The shrill sound of her cell phone breaks her away from me. Her eyes are wide when she pulls away, and her puffy lips look decadent. She picks up her phone and starts talking to the person on the other end. Her face falls, the darkness returns to her eyes, and I wish I could turn back time. I want to protect her from the world's devastating stings by wrapping her in a bubble of my love.

"Mom, I didn't know," her voice shrinks.

While she is on the phone, I tidy up after the dinner that we ate at the coffee table.

She hangs up the phone and looks at me, "I'm sorry. I've missed a lot of her calls." Her eyes don't meet mine.

"Let's talk it out. I'm not leaving until I know you're alright."

"It's nothing serious. It's just the way it is." She walks over to her favourite chair, and I flop down on the one across from it.

"It's not. People don't get to be shitty to you over and over. I know that there is a light inside of you because I've seen it."

"She said that I'm a selfish person who only cares about myself. She threw a party for my brother after he got his first promotion, but I couldn't attend. Like it matters, she pays for everything he has. I've gotten so many promotions, so many life events have passed by me, and she didn't give a shit. Why do I have to care about everyone else when no one cares about me? And to top it all off, she just blames me constantly for my trauma. She abused me forever, and it's my fault? How is that fair? How is any of this fair?" Tears fill her eyes, and my heart drops.

I move across the room quickly and kneel in front of her. I look into her eyes and lace my fingers with hers. "We could kill her," I whisper, wanting to erase anyone who has ever hurt her.

Her eyes widen in surprise but never leave mine as she processes my words. "That's crazy. We can't just kill her, can we?" It's like the idea never dawned on her, and that is one reason I love her so, her heart isn't filled to the brim with the dark sludge mine is.

"We can end her and your misery at the same time. Open up your life for happiness." Her lips part, a flash of something passes through her eyes that I don't recognize, and it's gone before I can even try to.

"I've always wanted to live in a world where either she or I don't exist, but I don't think I could do it. I'm flattered you would do that for me, though."

I think this is it. This is where she tells me that I'm too fucked up for her to love. She joins me on the floor and places her hands on either side of my face before she kisses me. Painfully aware of the hard floor under us, I break the kiss to pick her up and walk to her bedroom, laying my gorgeous dove on the bed. A sign of peace is what she is. She's the only sign I need in the universe to tell me I'm not alone.

As I remove her sweater, I feel the softness of the fabric against my fingertips. I don't want her to feel judged or embarrassed when she's with me. I rip the band tee I'm wearing off and watch her eyes run over my lean body.

My lips meet and wrestle with hers, and I can feel the intensity of our passion growing. She breaks the kiss, and the sound of the zipper echoes as she shimmies out of her jeans. I roll onto my back, and she positions herself on top of me, straddling my body. Her warmth grinds on my leg, and her gaze fills with desire. I run my hands over her smooth skin. Her lips find mine again, and I slide my fingers into her panties. Marla's wetness coats her slit, and I run the pad of my thumb over her clit and ease my middle digit into her. I fuck her slowly with my fingers, my mouth capturing every moan and the scream that dies on my lips.

She smirks before she moves off of me, laying her head on my chest. My dick aches, but her face on my chest is all I need at this moment. I'll have lots of time to fuck her silly. "That was great," she whispers against my skin.

"It's only the beginning," I tell her as we fall asleep.

"You are too late." I stare at Clyde, and my mouth dries.

"What the fuck do you mean? I'm a day behind." His dead eyes stare back at me, but tonight, he's not high like normal. I've spent so much time with Marla that I've slipped on my usual jobs. He puts his hand on the door frame, and his stained wife beater grips his body. "Yeah, too late. I'll get someone else."

As I throw my shoulder into his chest, he stumbles back out of the door into his shitty apartment. I close the door behind me. "What the fuck, man?"

I act on instinct and punch him in the face. I can feel the bones in his nose give way beneath my strength as blood flows. As I scan his cluttered living room, my eyes dart around, searching for his phone or a phone nummber.

"Who's your supplier?" Gritting my teeth, I knock everything off his coffee table. A knife catches my eye, and I grab the handle.

"If you think I'm just going to let you take my spot, you are fucking stupid," he spits at me as I turn to face him.

"Oh, but I think you will. I'll slit your throat right now, and you can bleed all over the filth you live in. Live and die in the same shithole that was always meant to destroy you." His eyes widen at the sight of the knife in my hand. He doesn't hesitate to pick up his phone and call someone.

"Yeah, I have someone who wants direct contact. He's been a dealer for me for years; he's the best sober dealer I've ever had," he jabbers on for a few minutes, ending the call as he looks at me. "Done. Here is his number, but don't fuck around because they won't be as forgiving."

I call the number myself and listen to the man on the other end set up a meeting between us for tomorrow.

"I did what you wanted. Now get the fuck out of my apartment. Just because you are a good dealer doesn't mean you get to be a psychotic bag of shit."

How wrong he is. I charge towards him and slip the knife across his throat. He falls to the floor, and I search for a container in the kitchen. My plants need to be fed, and I didn't have the leisure of bringing him home. Sifting through cupboards, I grab a large thermos and place it next to him and fill it with his essence.

While I wipe my prints off everything I've touched, I look around for cash and take half of what he has. His bathroom smells like a bad truck stop, and I do my best to breathe from my mouth as I examine my appearance for blood and wash my hands.

On my way out the door, I grab the thermos and walk to my car to put it in the trunk. I don't have a lot of time until the blood might spoil, and I have to bury the bodies that no doubt are stinking up the shed by now. My phone vibrates in my pocket. I have one more appointment before I have to get home.

"Mr. York, I'm hopeful you are still coming today." Shit, I'm late.

"Yes, I'll be there in about five minutes. Sorry, I had another business meeting that went too long." After I get into the car, I drive to the other side of town into an office parking lot. Walking into the real estate office, I feel underdressed, but it shouldn't matter.

"Mr. York, I assume?" the man in the suit asks. I nod. "Follow me. My office is just over here." We walk a short distance and enter a small room with beige walls. There are a couple of chairs on one side of the desk and his on the other. "Have a seat. We shouldn't be long. I just need you to sign a few forms. We have your down payment already, just the final dotted I's,"

I smile as I read over the files. "Excellent." I jot my initials on the dotted line.

"Congratulations, you are now the owner of Clancy Court Apartments."

Shaking his hand for the last time, I take the folder and smile before I'm out the door on my way home. Now I can make sure there won't be another creepy landlord around my Marla. While I drive home, I think about the work ahead of me, the hole needs to be dug, and the plants need to be fed. I hope I'll have enough time left to visit her. I feel like my chest is collapsing because I haven't seen her in a day.

As I pull into the driveway, I go straight to work, feeding the plants. With the thermos in hand, I make my way to the shed. My intuition was correct. The bodies are worse for wear in the couple weeks I've been away. I should have thought of an excuse to come home sooner, but I didn't want to leave her. I grab the shovel and head out to the yard, choosing a small piece of the backyard that the rain has already softened. More flowers will have to be planted to mask the sight of the last hole.

Once I've dumped the pieces of bodies into the Earth, I cover it with dirt and put away my tools. Since time is still on my side, I walk into the house and shower before grabbing a pair of jeans and a black band tee and getting dressed quickly. Doing a last glance around, I make sure everything is in place and drive back into town.

Nine

Marla

Sebastian wasn't at the centre today, and I worry that he'll get a fine. The reason for his absence is unknown. I wasn't close to having my number called by the time the centre closed. The day was uneventful without him next to me. In the last month, we've hung out every day, and I know in my heart that I'm falling for him. His witty comebacks, the way he takes care of me, how handsome he is, and his muscular arms around me when we cuddle is my favourite spot in the world.

He makes me feel like I'm worth something, that I'm irreplaceable. My entire life, I've been picked over. Everyone would rather have someone else, even my family. No one has ever wanted to see the real me. He changes things for me and gives me the strength to continue. He makes me feel when I'm usually numb, and since we've spent more time together, I haven't slid the blade over my skin. The scars that line my arms make me embarrassed, but he never makes me take off my shirt. He isn't someone who would judge me.

A new girl passed me on my way out of the centre today. When I saw her long blonde hair twisted in a frizzy mess it made me want to help her brush it out. For the first time in a long time I feel I can help someone else, like Sebastian does for me. But all I can do is offer her a smile, my mind unable to make up the words and talk to her.

The chill in the air cuts through my sweater as I walk home, my head down until I reach my apartment. I check my phone, but there are no messages from him. Fear enters my body without my permission. I wonder if I'm too much work. Maybe he doesn't want to be around me anymore. My breath catches in my throat while a fog clouds my mind. If everyone thought I wasn't worth the effort, why would a guy think I was?

I lay on my bed, ignoring the calls from my mother. She'll only cut me deeper than the demons in my head. I look at the wall until my tears stop, rearranging doubt and letting the pieces settle. I hear rapid knocks at the door, and as I walk to the entrance, I worry it'll be my creepy landlord.

"My dove, what happened?" His deep brown eyes look into mine fiercely, taking in my crumpled appearance.

"I'm sorry," is all I can whisper. My tears return, and I do my best to blink them away.

"Never apologize. You did nothing wrong. What happened?" He closes the door and walks towards me until my back hits the wall. One hand leans above me as he looks down into my eyes. His body wash wraps around me as he leans closer, his hand strokes my cheek.

"It's stupid," I get out.

"Nah, not you. Not possible. Who hurt you?"

"My mind. I worried that you'd had enough of me. That you were sick of taking care of me and left, and I couldn't contain how it made me feel."

His eyes soften as he drops his face to mine. He's so close, his breath is on my skin. "Never. You are everything I have ever wanted in my entire life. You are my moon, the sky, and all the fucking stars. I will never leave you unless you tell me to. Even then, I won't really leave." He kisses my tears away from my cheeks, and his mouth moves to mine.

My hands wrap around his waist, and we stand in the entranceway together. His forehead presses to mine as he breaks the kiss. "What we have is rare. You quiet my thoughts, Marla. You are the peanut butter to my jam, the only person I feel like I can be myself around."

Before I can say anything, my phone is ringing again. His eyes bore into mine. He leans back and kisses my forehead as I answer. "Hello, Mother," I say.

"Finally! What if it was an emergency? What if I was dying? What if I needed you, and you were too selfish to answer the fucking phone?" she screams into the phone.

My eyes meet Sebastian's, and he offers me a half smile and holds up his smokes. I nod, listening to her endless shit while we walk out for a cigarette. "Are you smoking? Marla, you know that will put you into an early grave."

"One could only hope, Mother. How are you?"

"You have to come over for dinner tomorrow night. I'd like to apologize in person."

I mute the phone and look at Sebastian. "Will you come to dinner tomorrow night at my mother's?" He grimaces but nods and then grins. "Hey, Mom, can I bring my friend?" If you could hear shock, it would be on repeat at this moment.

"You have a friend? Who is this person?" Her judgmental tone sounds like she doesn't believe me.

"His name is Sebastian. He's more than a friend but not quite a boyfriend." Hope blooms in my chest. It feels like what we have is far beyond a normal relationship, but I wouldn't know what to call us.

"Yes, I guess that is fine. I'll make the adjustments to the size of portions. You really could have let me know in advance so I wouldn't have to go to so much trouble," she scoffs.

"Well, I don't eat that much, so he could share with me, or we could bring tacos for dinner."

"What have you become? A fucking heathen?"

Ah, of course, maybe it is a bad idea to bring him. If he found out the level of hate I come from, he might run like the wind. Picking at the hole in my jeans, I listen to her talk down to me. Sebastian covers my hand with his own and shakes his head, pulling me from the dark place in my mind.

"Alright, Mother, we will be there tomorrow at five," I tell her. I hang up and turn my head to Sebastian.

"It'll be alright. Together we are stronger," he says, and I wonder how he can be optimistic, but it's because he's never met her. She is the type to drain the will to live from your veins and blame you for making her do it.

"Hopefully you are right, I don't have to go to the centre tomorrow, but you will have to get your fine. Other than work, I don't have any plans."

"Me either. I have a few days off work until they are finished changing management."

"Can you give my hair a trim tonight?" He grins and nods. Jumping up, he brings his chair into the kitchen, and I grab the scissors from the bathroom.

This time, I'm much more relaxed as he brushes my hair and does his magic. It's so much easier than struggling through the panic of a new hairdresser and salon.

When he's finished, I have a quick shower as he cleans up. Grabbing a long-sleeved metal tee, I slip it over my head and pull on plaid shorts.

"Want to watch a movie?" he asks as I enter the living room. I grab the remote and hand it to him as I sit with him on the chair.

His hands trace a tantalizing path over my body as we watch the plot unfold. Tilting my head up, I meet his lips with mine, the sensation sending a shiver down my spine. As his hand slides up my body, I feel his firm grip around my throat while our kiss intensifies. I straddle him, feeling the heat of his body beneath me as our tongues dance. Sebastian's hand slips into my shorts. He finds my clit quickly and rubs me gently as I grow wet for him. He pulls away from me to open his pants, wets his lips and looks into my eyes. The last few times we've hooked up has only been about me, and when I pull out his hard dick, I'm surprised to see the silver piercings down his shaft.

"Did this hurt?" I ask, realizing that's probably a stupid question.

"It did at first, but not now. If you aren't comfortable going further, we can do something else." Running my fingers down over the bars, the groan that he lets out fills me with need. I stand to pull my shorts off and then hover over him, lowering myself down slowly. I feel every ridge as he enters me. His hands grip my hips tightly as I take all of him.

"Fuck, this is better than I would have ever imagined," he says as his eyes lower over the front of us. Holding onto his shoulders, I ride him at my pace. One of his hands moves between us, his thumb strokes my clit, and his other hand grabs me by the throat as he pumps into me.

"Sebastian, I'm going to come," I whisper as the pleasure courses through my body. The way his eyes look into mine, as if he wants to devour me, sends me over the edge. He stands without putting me down and walks me to my bedroom. My back hits the comforter as he lowers me and fucks into me harder.

"You feel incredible. I'm not going to last." He hooks his arm under my leg, and the angle sets fire to my body and spots cover my eyes as I come again, harder than I ever have in my life. He doesn't stop, and soon he pulls out, lifts my shirt, and comes over my stomach. "My sweet dove, that was incredible."

I turn my head and look at his sweaty face, biting the inside of my lip, emotions swirl through me. I lean over to kiss his cheek before I get up to clean up in the bathroom. We fall asleep quickly when I return.

Ten

Sebastian

As I walk up to her door to pick her up for dinner with her mother, my nerves swirl in my stomach. The thought of her mother not liking me doesn't worry me. I'm more certain of that than anything. I'm worried about Marla and what effect tonight will have on her.

As I knock, the door opens and my breathing almost stops. Marla is dressed in a simple black dress, the sleeves halfway down her forearms, and it cuts off around her knee. Her hair is straight, red lipstick adorns her lips, she has leather cuffs on both wrists and red gemstones grace her ears. She is a vision of perfection. I want to take her away and protect her from everything that may come.

"Sebastian, you look great. Do you want to come in while I order an Uber?"

I look down at my dark jeans and t-shirt and wonder what she sees. Lifting my sunglasses onto my head, I step forward and draw her in for a kiss. My hand cups her lower back, and her hand falls against my chest.

"I have a car." This surprises her. I wait while she grabs her purse, and we're out the door.

"I'll give you her address," she says, rattling off the address, and I roughly know where we're heading. "I'd rather walk anywhere with you than drive, but this is too far to walk." I laugh and link my fingers with hers as we walk to the car.

"How was your day?" I ask her as we drive to her mother's.

"It was good. I got a lot of projects done. I had a meeting, and one of my clients wants to take me on full-time," her smile lights up the car. "How was yours?"

"I'm so incredibly proud of you. All your talent and hard work is finally being recognized. My day was alright, just took care of some gardening." We drive in comfortable silence. My hand never leaves her knee until we pull into the driveway.

When we get out of the car, I put my arm around her waist. The short walk to the door is all the time needed for Marla's entire body to tense under my touch.

"This house has a heavy cloud of despair over it," I whisper, and Marla gives me a meek smile.

She presses the doorbell, and I lower my hand to squeeze hers. Her reaction to coming here breaks my heart.

"She won't like me, but that's not my problem. You are incredible, and you need to remember that," I whisper as we wait.

A middle-aged woman with pin-straight, dark brown hair appears. She has green eyes and awful square glasses that don't match her face, which is heavily caked in makeup. "Oh, you must be Sebastian. Nice to meet you. I'm Violet." She doesn't offer her hand, and I don't stick mine out. I'm almost certain we've crossed paths before, maybe years ago, when she looked younger and had a more natural appearance.

"Nice to meet you, ma'am." Her eyes stare at me in disdain, but she holds her tongue.

"Glad to see you can dress up, Marla." My dove flinches, her mother's words are meant to cut and hurt.

As we walk up the stairs, I look around. Large chestnut china cabinets line the walls, filled to the brim with knickknacks and pictures. I see none of Marla, which is unfortunate. Walking to the kitchen, the smell of steamed vegetables hangs in the air. "I hope you both are hungry. I've been working hard again. I made vegetables, rice and a chicken recipe I found online."

Marla's eyes fall on the dishes. "Thank you, Mom. You didn't have to go through all this trouble."

"Of course I did. It's not every day that you come over with a man. How did you guys meet? Oh, my manners. Can I get you anything to drink?" her eyes are on me.

"Water, please." She pulls two bottles out and hands one to Marla and the other to me.

"Glasses?" I shake my head to say no before we dish up dinner and bring it to the table.

"How is Ashley doing with her new job?" Marla asks. Her mother shakes her head, with a slight eye roll.

"Call her and ask if you are so concerned. So where did you guys meet? Because you don't go anywhere, Marla. Was it one of those internet dating sites? I've told you they aren't meant for you."

I roll my tongue over my lip ring, darting my eyes to Marla. Her eyes are on her plate, a slight pink hue over her cheeks. "No, we met at a coffee shop near her place. I mistakenly took her order and when I saw her, I couldn't resist asking her for her number."

I shovel a forkful of cauliflower into my mouth. The vegetables taste bland and devoid of any flavour. In an instant, it all comes together in my mind and I recall the familiar face of her mother. She used to be a customer back when I first started dealing. She really loved Valium and Xanax. I had a lot less tattoos back then, so I wonder if she recognizes me.

"That's nice. Have you been keeping your apartment clean, Marla?" She diverts her eyes to me before speaking again. "She has trouble with basic tasks. Sometimes I feel like I'm babysitting her more than I should."

I don't want to leave Marla alone, but if I sit at this table another minute, I'm going to shred her mother's throat with my knife.

"Bathroom?" I ask.

"Down the hall, third door on the right." Her mother's smile is as fake as she is. It's no wonder Marla is always on edge. Growing up on eggshells moulds a person. It replaces forming a functioning adult with a surviving human.

As I tuck my chair under the table, I run my fingers over the back of Marla's neck, tracing the delicate curve. When I'm out of her mother's sight, I quickly form a heart shape with my hands.

Once in the bathroom, I stand in front of the mirror and do my best to reign in my anger. Turning on the faucet, I splash water on my face and count backward from fifty. Easing open the door, I stroll back to the kitchen, hearing the tail end of the conversation.

"You have to end this. You can't be with someone like that. What the fuck is wrong with you besides the obvious?" Her voice drips with malice. I hate her more than I've hated most people.

"Sebastian is a good man. He keeps me safe and treats me like the adult I am."

"Oh, this bullshit again. Yes, Marla, you are an adult. There I said it, are you happy now? You can fucking end this piss poor excuse of a relationship."

"No. I'm falling for him. Sebastian makes me feel like I matter, like I'm worth something."

Her mother scoffs, but doesn't let up. "He'll tire of you, quickly. You are not worth the effort."

"I don't believe you. He won't tire of me. We have something special." My little dove is a fighter. I'll do everything in my power to make her feel seen, heard, and appreciated.

"Fine, if you don't end it with him, I'll end myself. Remember the last time you pulled this sort of shit? It'll be the real deal this time. Is that what you want? I'll tell everyone that you could have prevented this."

I walk a little heavier into the kitchen and the conversation ceases. "Are you guys going to stick around for dessert? It's been such a pleasure meeting you, Sebastian."

"No, thank you. We have to be going. I have to get to work." Marla looks up at me, her eyes lined with tears for a person who doesn't deserve them. "Let's go, Marla." I hold out my hand and she grips my fingers tightly.

"Nice to meet you, Violet," I wave as we walk out the door, taking a deep inhale of the night air.

"I'm sorry," Marla whispers.

"Nope. You don't get to be sorry." We get into the car, and I drive us back to town.

"Tacos?" she smiles and I know the next stop we'll make. "Does she make the threat often that she'll kill herself? That's a crazy manipulation trick."

"You heard the conversation?" she asks. I can only nod.

We reach the taco shop and I place our order to go. After about ten minutes, I walk it back to the car. Holding up the bag, I ask her, "Tacos and British comedies?"

She laughs, and it's music to my ears. Anger and disappointment for her shitty mother run through me and I need to turn the night around. "I'd rather just have tacos and talk."

"What do you want to talk about?" I ask her, focusing on the road as I drive back to her apartment.

"Is the offer still on the table?" she asks. I think about it for a minute, wondering what she means. "The offer to kill her?" she clarifies, and I give her a wicked grin.

"Always. Anyone for you." She doesn't say anything until we're in her apartment. I don't want to expose the truth about myself unless she is truly ready to go ahead with this.

"How would we do it?" Her question bounces around inside my head as we lay out the tacos on the coffee table, sitting across from each other on the floor. Excitement runs through her eyes. I want to give her all the power. "What happened before?"

"She didn't like my first boyfriend and threatened to kill herself. Told everyone it would be my fault if she did it. I didn't break up with him and she sent me her suicide note and disappeared for a few days. When I broke up with him, she reappeared and then her words got worse for a while."

I stare at her. "That is fucked. That is next level fucked." She doesn't say anything, and we eat in silence for a while. I think over what she's said, and my stomach drops for how she must have felt. "Do you still have the note?"

"Yeah, somewhere. She dropped it in my mail-box. Is that how we could do it?"

I nod, knowing it won't be a huge mess, which she probably doesn't want to see. "We could stage a suicide, if you can stand another dinner with her."

She nods as she looks down at her phone. "Thank you. I really need this. Her love for me has always been nonexistent, and our relationship has been constantly negative. It's clear that things will never change. If she didn't exist, then I think I could finally heal."

It's all I want for her. While she cleans up from dinner, I grab two cigarettes, walk outside, and light them.

"I know this is the right move. It makes me feel hopeful, almost giddy. Like I can't believe I'm going to get back my life and re-take my power from her." She bites her lip and looks incredibly sexy as she takes a drag and looks into my eyes.

"All I want is for you to feel the best you can. Thank you for sticking up for me. No one ever has." She stubs out her smoke and grabs my hand. I barely have time to flick mine into the ashtray. "I want to show you how appreciative I am."

We don't stop until we're in her bedroom. She pulls her dress off and her lithe body is so perfect I could shed a tear. This is the first time she's bared herself to me entirely.

I rip my shirt over my head as I walk towards her. My hands cup either side of her face as my lips meet hers. Her arms wrap around my back, drawing me closer. Pulling away from her, I feather kisses along her jawline, dipping my head to her neck.

Her nails dig into my back as she lets out a soft moan. As we move backward, I guide her until her back touches the wall, and then I kneel in front of her. I gaze into Marla's eyes, desire ignites within them as I trail kisses along her thighs, drawing closer to her panties. I hook my fingers into the sides and pull them down her legs, lifting one to rest on my shoulder as I explore her. With her hand tightly gripping my hair, I bring my mouth closer to her core, parting her with my tongue. As I delve deeper, I inhale her sweet scent.

"Yes, please. Fuck," she mumbles as I lick her slit, using my hand to open her further. I fuck her with my tongue, rubbing her clit with my thumb. I lick her until her thighs tremble and she's coming all over my tongue.

"Beautiful," I say through my gritted teeth. I'm painfully hard and want to fuck her. As I stand, I turn her around, pressing her against the wall. I quickly undo my belt and drop my pants. I slide into her, slowly allowing her to get used to the size, and then I fuck her harder. My hand snakes around to her throat, holding her in place as I slam into her. My other hand roams over her perfect tits. Having her at my mercy is one thing I've ached to have for so fucking long. Her body tenses and she comes all over my cock.

I drag myself out of her tightness. "Get on your knees for me, Marla." She turns and obeys. Her mouth explores the head of my dick, but I'm so close to the edge I can't handle it. I put my fingers through her hair and slide into her mouth. Her tongue is everywhere, and I lose it in the back of her throat.

"So, fucking perfect," I breathe heavily as I pull her up. Dipping my head, I kiss her. Tasting us both in her mouth might be my favourite flavour. "I really fucking like you, my dove."

She smiles and bites her lip as she turns away to grab a shirt from her drawer. "I really fucking like you," she says before walking out of the room.

Marla

It's been a week of playing the same game with my mother: the makeup game. Text messages and calls to pretend I'm the dutiful perfect daughter that she can control so perfectly. It isn't so hard, I've been that way my entire life. But this is the first time I've really wanted to stand up for what is best for me. Sebastian is what I need in my life. He makes the demons in my head fade away. The darkness inside of me isn't as active with him around.

The thought of killing her seemed ludicrous at first, but it was planted like a little seed in the back of my mind, and every time she would dig at me, the words that cut my soul a little more, the seed grew until that dinner with him and the way she acted. Talking about me like I was a child in front of him, saying horrible things about him. I'm sure she's already messaged the family text thread that she is going to off herself.

I found the note from the last time and, as I think of what might happen, my stomach rolls. All I've ever wanted was for her to be proud of me, acknowledge all the pain she's caused me and apologize but I know she isn't capable of remorse, or change.

I've been at the mental health centre most of the day, going over everything in my head, overthinking every angle. Sebastian said that he will drop me off near her house and wait for me to text him that I've dropped the light sedative in her drink. Today feels like an eternity as the hours sluggishly crawl by. The gravity of the situation is setting in. This is really going to happen. Bursting with excitement, every second feels like a lifetime. The air in the centre is saturated with the sharp, chemical smell of aseptic cleaner, which becomes suffocating as the day goes on.

"It smells terrible in here today. I mean, sure, sometimes it smells like no one showers, or has pissed their pants, but this is by far the worst." The voice comes from the girl I saw last week. Her long blonde hair is braided today and a black hoodie hangs off her. It's far too warm out to be wearing one, but I don't question it.

"I'm Marla. Nice to meet you." I know we aren't supposed to be in here making friends, but I keep my voice hushed.

"I'm Jess. Nice to meet you. Well, as nice as being here can be." I nod.

"How long have you been coming here?" she asks.

I think for a minute. "I think about six months." Her eyes widen, likely thinking the same thing I do every day. I'm never going to get the fucking help I need.

"I'm sorry. I hope they call your number soon." Just as the words are out of her mouth, the lady stands with the PA system and says they are done for the day.

"Or not. It's alright. I'll see you next time. Have a good night," I tell her as I leave through the door before the mob of people chokes up the exit.

As I walk home, my mind races. What if Mother suspects something, or what if the cops realize it's not suicide and put me away for life? Will I really be able to do this?

"Marla." My eyes focus on Sebastian. He's just standing there in front of my apartment.

"What are you doing here?" I ask him. I'm thankful he's here, but we didn't have plans for another hour. Unlocking my door, I let him in, and he sits down on the chair.

"I had some business, so I figured I'd stop by to wait for you. Sorry you didn't get your number called today."

"Yeah, it is what it is. I talked to that new girl. Her name is Jess." He doesn't say anything. I walk to my bedroom to get changed for tonight.

"Pack a spare, just in case," he tells me from the doorway, his body leans against the frame. He's wearing a Billy Talent band tee and old jeans, his hat backwards and all his bracelets are gone from his wrists.

"Okay. Do you have the drug?"

He pulls a small bag out of his pocket. "Crushed it so you don't have to worry."

I narrow my eyes, take a deep breath, and put on the clothes. "We don't have to do this. It isn't too late to back out," he says as he enters the room and wraps his arms around me, kissing my shoulder.

"No, we can't. I want this. Will she be right out or still awake?"

"Still awake, but I can get more." I shake my head.

"No, I want her awake. She needs to shut up for five seconds and listen to me."

He kisses my forehead and grabs my bag of clothes. Without a word, he turns on his heels and walks out the door. I check my phone and see her message. I'm almost late for her dinner. "Let's go."

As I walk down the road, the bag practically burns in my pocket. I think about the decades of abuse, the fact she will never change, and the years she swept things under the rug because it was just me. I ruminate on how little I matter to her, the way she blamed me for so many things going wrong in her life. I remember when I went to her, telling her about her friend taking advantage of me and how he would touch me in ways I didn't want, and she ignored me. The words, the manipulation, the lies, the names, the lack of love.

Reaching the door, I'm reminded as soon as I see her fake smile, why I'm really here. "I guess you only dress up when you have that man around. Glad you came back to me and to make nice."

I smile as sweetly as I can. This person standing in front of me was supposed to show me the way of life. She was meant to be a role model to me, but instead became fuel for nightmares, and caused years of trauma that hold me down within myself.

"I have been super busy. It's that time of year for the lawns and stuff, so I only had time to make sandwiches," she titters on as we walk up the stairs.

"It's perfect. Did you stop using the lawn care people?"

"No, they were here today, but it's my job to direct them," she says sharply. I roll my eyes, as if the workers couldn't have done their jobs without her direction. We sit at the table, across from each other. "I'm so glad you came to your senses. You know how you get, you fall head over heels for someone who doesn't return the sentiment, and then I'll be the one to deal with you."

I nod. "I usually fall too hard and get too attached to someone. It's a crazy thing seeking validation from other people."

"It's about time you had some insight. You aren't like other girls, Marla. It's just not in the cards for you to fall in love. Love isn't meant for you. I wish you could have had what your father and I had, but you aren't like me," she smiles. It sours my stomach, another gut punch with words.

"I'll get the sandwiches. You must be tired from today," I say as I stand.

"Thank you. It's nice of you to start caring again. It's all I've ever wanted from you. Just that love and respect you are supposed to give your parents. Grab my drink, it's in the fridge."

I grit my teeth. I've spent my entire life trying to prove my love to her. All I've ever done in life is show her that I was worth something, anything. For her to acknowledge me and be proud enough to love. Her words cut me like a thousand blades. I empty the bag into her drink and watch as it dissolves.

As I walk back to the table, I put down her drink and sandwich and then go back to the kitchen and get my sandwich and a bottle of water. I watch her drink and I nibble on the bread and break apart the cheese to eat.

"Why must you play with your food? You are a grown adult." Her eyes blaze into mine. The anger behind them is undeniable.

The mask slips for a little longer than usual. "Who can see us? Does it matter how I eat?" I ask her. At this rate, I don't even care if the drugs don't work. I've reached the end of my rope and if I hold on any tighter, I'm going to hurt myself.

"No, but it's disgusting. You could have dirty hands. See? I told you that you are an adult again. Happy?" Her eyes still blaze with anger, but her lips are more lax than normal. She moves her arm to hold her head up.

"No, Mom, I'm not happy. I haven't been happy in a long time, but I think that is exactly what you want."

Her mask isn't back. There's no more fake smile across her face. Instead, what resembles a sneer is in its place. My fingers move swiftly across the screen of my phone as I text Sebastian. He won't have any problems entering since I forgot to lock the door behind us. "What. Did. You. Do?" Her words are clipped, with a pause between each one. Her eyes look less bright, and she is struggling to sit upright.

"What did I miss?" Sebastian asks as he enters the kitchen. Her eyes dart to him and she hisses.

"Not much. But whatever was in that bag has made her furious."

"Oh no, my sweet. That isn't the drug, that's the real her. The drug just fades away the exterior she puts on for everyone. Let's get her up. Bathroom or her bedroom?"

I think about which will mean less mess for when I will probably have to come back and deal with this, as the grieving daughter. "Bathtub if we can." He nods, lowering his sleeves. He puts on gloves that he retrieves from his pockets. Without hesitation, he takes her to the bathroom.

I clean up the plates from dinner, then wash and rinse her glass. As I walk into the bathroom, she is sitting upright in the bathtub, fully clothed. She stares at me but she doesn't say anything.

"It's up to you. You can say your piece and leave, or you can do the honours." Sebastian holds up the blade. I look into his eyes. There is no judgement in them. He honestly would do whatever I wanted. I reach for the blade.

Grasping one of her forearms, I drag the sharp edge from her wrist to her elbow. Letting it drop before her toxic blood can touch me, I follow up with the other. The blood runs out of each wound faster than I would have thought. I'm mesmerized by it, by the way her breathing slows. Her eyes stare at me and I feel alive. For the first time in over twenty years, the darkness pulls back fully from my eyes, my mind is quiet, and the worry is gone.

"Listen to me Mother. All I ever wanted was for you to love me. That is all. You love Michael and Ashley with such fierceness, I always wondered why not me. Why couldn't you love me? What have I ever done to you? Since I was a child you've treated me differently, for my entire life I've had to live under your shadow, be the good one. Don't rock the boat, don't cause a scene." She stares at me, withholding the words I ache to hear even as she stands upon death's door.

"You're just as useless as I always knew you were," her voice is barely a whisper.

"We'll never know why you treated me that way, but the world is a better place without you in it. I've had to fight for so long, you never even gave me a chance. You proved over and over that I wasn't worthy of love. I gave you every effort. I tried so hard, and for what? Someone to beat me down further. Why wasn't I good enough for you to love?" The tears wet my face before I realize I'm crying. The release from ending her life is far superior to marking myself.

"Give me the blade. It's okay. You did so well," Sebastian says quietly.

I watch as he wipes my prints off of the handle and puts it in her hand, it falls to the porcelain tub that is covered in crimson swirls, some of it has gone down the drain, leaving a metallic smell in the air. I exit the room, my footsteps echoing through the hallway.

Retrieving the letter, I examine it for a date, but find none. I set it down gently on the bench among the neatly stacked towels. "Do you think we should check her phone?" I ask him.

He looks at me and nods. I grab it from the table to check her messages, but nothing has been sent since last week when she told everyone if I didn't get my shit together, I was going to give her a heart attack. I roll my eyes and wipe my prints off her phone, laying it in her bedroom.

"You are handling this pretty well. Are you sure you're okay?" He looks at me. I think it over for a minute, purse my lips and nod.

"Do you need anything?" He looks over the scene and back at me.

"Two things."

"Whatever you want, your wish is my command."

"They both sound fucking crazy." I bite my lip, thinking my thoughts over in my head.

He laughs lightly. "Your wish is my command," he repeats himself.

"Well, I want to fuck. I can't explain why, but I just do. And then I want to show you the memories of the house." He nods, stalking towards me.

Dropping the gloves on the floor, he lowers his lips to mine. The kiss is hard, and I match his energy, our lips battling each other like we're trying to become one. He turns me to face the sink, my hands on the counter as he rips down my pants, tearing my panties off swiftly. But he is slower to slide into me. Every inch slides in slowly. The wall blocks the bathtub, but I know she's on the other side and I couldn't think of a better fuck you than this. With that thought, a moan escapes my mouth and I look up into the mirror, watching Sebastian's face focused on where we are joined.

"Fuck, you are so fucking perfect," he grits out as he begins to pound into me. I lean my head down to take the thrusts and grip the edge of the sink as I fall over the edge, clenching down on his cock as I come.

Twelve

Sebastian

I pull her ponytail, forcing her head up to watch in the mirror. I want to look into her hazel eyes when I come inside her. One hand grips her hip as I wrap my hand around her hair. "Fuck. Come for me again. Drench my cock. I'm so fucking close." I watch her face contort in ecstasy as she comes again. As she clenches down tightly on me, everything is too much, and I slam into her harder and fill her.

"So, fucking perfect. I love you." The words escape my lips before I can think about what I've said, the lack of blood in my head.

"I love you too," she utters the words I've always wanted to hear from her perfect mouth. But I take them with a grain of salt. It's an eventful night and I don't want to believe she loves me unless it's true.

After we're situated, I look down at her beautiful face. "What's next, the memories?"

She bites her lip, glancing around. "I don't know how this will work. I didn't think about the note." Her eyebrows knit together, and worry crosses her face.

"Tell me. We'll figure it out."

As we walk down the hall, she leads me into a cluttered bedroom. "This is the room she let me be touched in when I didn't want it." She walks back out to the living room and points to the pristine couch. "This is where I wasn't allowed to sit because I'm so dirty. I had to squat next to it whenever I was bad." She uses quotation fingers.

My blood is still boiling over the first confession that someone touched her and the fact that her cunt of a mother let it happen.

"The kitchen is where she had me count calories. She wasn't happy with herself, but she hated me more. Could we burn the house down?" Her gaze is unfocused until she looks at me.

"In due time, but for now, I think it's best for the family to find the note and for this to look as authentic as possible. I do promise we will, though."

She follows me as I go through the house for any signs we were here. It's fine if they know she was here, and I'll give them the alibi that I picked her up.

"Right. The note, the family. I'm so fucking stupid." I stop moving and she slams into my back. I turn and grip her by her throat and pin her against the wall.

"No, you aren't stupid, and you won't become a reflection of this cunt who spit those words at you." Looking down into her eyes, I let her go, and she continues to follow me out of the house. I look over at her as we get into the car. "I won't let you talk shit about yourself. In my eyes, you are the most precious human being I've ever met, an oddity that I get the pleasure to enjoy. And the power you hold over me? Pfft. I'd do anything you ask."

We make a quick pit stop at the taco place, and she scurries inside to grab our food. The only sound in the car is the hum of the engine as we drive home. The tip of the cigarette glows red as I light it, and take a deep drag.

I worry about her. Your first kill is exhilarating, but it can also tear you apart. After I killed my father, I was a mess for months until the urge came back. Since then I haven't looked back, but not everyone is like me. It may be the same for her. Killing your parents is harder than killing a stranger. It doesn't matter how evil they are, you hope and pray that they will start loving you at some point in your life. But they never do and you're just left with residue from the abuse, the trauma from every action they played out on you, and being emotionally stunted. You are left with work to do while they portray themselves as the innocent victims.

"You handling everything alright?" I ask her as I park the car. We get out of the vehicle and walk to her apartment.

"Yeah, it's just surreal. I've wanted this for so long and, now that it's done, it doesn't feel like anything happened." I say nothing as I watch her unlock the door and we go into her apartment.

We change and get settled on the couch to eat our dinner. I keep glancing over at her. "I told you, I'm alright. It'll just take a bit of time." My hand glides smoothly over her back, tracing the curve of her spine. She's everything I've ever wanted and watching her kill sealed the deal for me. I want to be with her forever.

"I am super exhausted, though. I didn't think that would happen."

As I stand, I tell her. "Go have a hot shower and get into bed. I'll clean up." She smiles at me and walks to the bathroom. As I hear the water going, I tidy up the garbage in her apartment from dinner and the past week. She tries her best, but I much prefer it when I clean for her. Finishing up around the same time she's getting into bed, I strip off my clothes and get in with her. Her warm body presses against mine and I put my hand over hers, holding her close.

"Goodnight, my dove." I press a kiss on her temple, listening to her breathing slow. I know she's asleep. She's the only person I want next to me for the rest of my life, together we can do anything.

It's been a week, and Marla has heard nothing. I'm surprised by how much her mother bragged about her other two children. I thought they would be there right away, but it took them much longer than I would have expected. Marla's phone rings relentlessly on the coffee table as we finish dinner.

"It's my sister. I wonder if this is it?" I look at her intently as she answers the phone.

"Hey, Ashley slow down. What happened?" She paces as she listens to what her sister is telling her, and her eyes sweep towards me often. "Oh my god, that is terrible. What do we do now?" Marla chews on her lip as she listens further. "I'll be there as soon as I can." She ends the call and looks at me.

"They have already removed the body. There are a couple of detectives, and they want to talk to me. Ashley wants me to go to the house, but I don't have a way to get there."

I think about it for a few minutes, but from the messages we saw, she didn't seem to tell anyone that she was having dinner with Marla. "I'll drive you. We saw the messages, and she never said you broke up with me."

She nods, grabs her purse and I stand up with her. "I think it's best if you stay in the car. Or does that look suspicious? Oh fuck, my head is running away on me."

After we climb into the car, I reach my hand across to the passenger side, stroking her wrist with my thumb as I focus on the road. "Listen, the less you say, the easier it will be. You won't have to lie, which tangles you into a web where they could catch you."

Her hand touches mine and she lets out a deep breath. "What if they catch me in a lie? What will I do?"

"You deleted that message to me that night?" She nods and I think for a minute, we pull onto the road where her mother lived. "You came for dinner and then I picked you up because I had to work and couldn't attend the dinner. You can mention she seemed distant but wouldn't say anything. I'll fill in the rest: I picked you up and we grabbed tacos, and then we went home."

As we park in the driveway, I notice the two cop cars, a couple of other cars, and a man and woman standing in front of the house. "I have a receipt from when I got tacos the first time, which would be around the time I picked you up."

Thirteen

Marla

My eyes widen as I look at him. "I wanted to be thorough. I won't lose you." Without another thought, I lean over and kiss him, hyper-aware of the way my dark sweater's tag itches the back of my neck. I swallow the lump in my throat and open the door to the car and get out, walking towards Ashley and Michael.

"Do they have any information?" I ask. Feeling Sebastian behind me gives me strength I don't normally have.

"So far, just that mom killed herself. There was a note, but they took it in for evidence. They've taken her away and questioned both of us," Ashley tells me. She crosses her arms over her chest. Tears line both their faces. I think of all the abuse my mother put me through so I can drum up the same emotion.

Tears cloud my vision quickly. I feel conflicted, like I should be sad, but I'm not.

"Miss Lee? We would like to talk to you." A man wearing dress pants, a button-down, and a blazer comes out of the house and walks in my direction.

"That's the detective I talked to. He's nice," Michael offers, his shoulders square off and he stands taller as the detectives walk out.

"We're going to call a cleaner once they are done processing the scene. If you can come over to my house tomorrow, we'll go over all the plans for the funeral and everything," Ashley says, and I watch them each get into their cars and leave.

"Do I have to come down to the station?"

"No, we can do it here. My partner Dan can question your boyfriend and I'll take down notes from you. It's pretty clean cut here, but just doing our due diligence."

Fear prickles in my scalp. Casting a glance at Sebastian, he smiles at me and gives a slight nod of his head. "Alright, thank you. Detective, um…?"

"My apologies. My wife says I'd forget my head if it wasn't attached. I'm Detective Hoyer and my partner is Detective Loams."

We walk over to the fence line. "So your sister tells us you had dinner with your mother a week ago?"

"Yeah, we weren't getting along the best. She didn't like my boyfriend, but I was trying to make her happier."

Hoyer pulls out his notepad and scribbles in it. "What did you have for dinner?"

"Mom was tired from the day, so we had sandwiches. It was cheese and lunchmeat, nothing fancy. She seemed exhausted. I asked a few times what was wrong, but she said she was fine." I pick at a hangnail, wondering if I look suspicious but not knowing how to act normal without seeming weird.

"It happens to the best of us. What time did you go home?"

"Shortly after six-thirty, Sebastian picked me up after he was done with work. We got tacos and drove home. I would have never left her if I thought this was what would happen."

"That's the thing, when you know, it's usually too late. Sometimes, people don't want to be helped.

"One more question. Did it not seem odd to you that she didn't talk to you all week? We checked her phone and she didn't send any messages over the last week."

I glance into his eyes before looking away. "We had a delicate relationship. Sometimes she would ignore me for weeks at a time. It was a normal thing for us." When I look back at him, his eyes soften. He looks sad for a minute.

"I'm sorry. If you think of anything, you can reach me here." He hands me his business card. "And if you ever need anyone to talk to, here is a list of agencies that can help." He hands over the list and gives me a quick smile before walking over to his partner.

Sebastian heads over to me. He lowers his sunglasses and grasps my hand, pulling me to the car. "You did perfectly."

While we drive home, my nerves from talking to the detectives settle, and my body starts to relax. "How would you know that I did good?"

He doesn't look away from the road. "Because you're in the car with me." As we enter the apartment, my mind detaches from the situation, like I'm being pulled into myself from reality.

"Smoke?" Sebastian's dark brown eyes look at me. I follow him to the patio, sitting in the hard plastic chair.

"Is it supposed to feel this way?"

He exhales the smoke. Leaning back in the chair, his head is tilted back to the sky. "Sorta. It's hard to explain."

I take a drag and exhale, watching the smoke swirl in front of me. "Please try?"

"I don't want you to think differently of me. I adore you, my dove." I look over at him, but he doesn't look towards me. What could make me change the way I feel about him? "It will feel odd for a while. You will go through the same emotions, but it'll get easier."

"How do you know?" I ask, stubbing out my cigarette and looking in his direction.

This time he jumps up, grabbing both armrests on my chair, his face inches from mine, eyes penetrating into my soul. "Because my father was like your mother. Except he didn't use his tongue to drip venom into my veins. He used objects and his belt."

He lowers his face and grazes my lips with his. "We're both so broken," I whisper, and he sighs.

"Only as broken as you perceive. They can steal a lot from us, but they won't steal our spirit. It can be broken, it can be bent, hell, it can shatter. But you hold on to it as tight as you can because it lights the fire within."

I run my hands up his arms and he pulls me from the chair. "I want to show you how much I adore you, Marla."

Without another word, he guides me to the bedroom. His eyes don't leave mine as he lowers me to the bed. Bracing himself over me, he lowers his mouth to mine. He kisses me as if he wants to devour me. I give as much as I can. When he pulls away, I'm breathless.

He sits upright and takes off his hat and shirt with one motion. Opening the buttons on my sweater, he drags it off my body. He opens my belt and pulls off my jeans, lowering his head to graze kisses over my neck, switching to the light bite of his teeth.

"Marla, sometimes when I'm not with you, I feel like I can't breathe, like I need your scent near me to feel human." I run my hands through his hair as he continues down my body. Out of reach, he looks up at me as he slides his fingers under the band of my panties. He drags them down my body agonizingly slowly. His hands push open my legs and his hot breath between them sets my nerves ablaze.

"Sebastian, please."

He softly chuckles, then uses his fingers to open me up to his view. "My sweet, perfect pussy."

His mouth is on my clit, sucking me as he slides two fingers into me. Pressure builds, and I know I won't be far off. My mind focuses only on this moment as the rush of pleasure runs through me. Nothing matters except his lips on me, his hands touching my skin and our pleasure together. Before I can reach climax, he stops.

Standing, he pulls off his jeans and positions himself between my legs. Lining himself up, he sinks into me. I don't know if I'll ever get used to his dick. The barbells run over every spot inside me. Inch by inch, I melt under him. Once he's fully inside, my legs over his hips, he leans down, one hand next to my head and the other around my neck.

"Fuck, yes. Please let me come."

His eyes simmer with desire as he looks down at me. "Soon. You are so fucking beautiful under me." As he fucks me harder, I reach between us to touch my clit, chasing my release. His hand captures mine and holds it against the bed.

"Not yet. Just hold it," he commands. The pleasure courses through my body, my muscles tighten up, and I can feel the edge barrelling towards me. "When I say." Sebastian reminds me.

I'm going crazy, the pressure builds and waves of pleasure surround me but don't take me under as he continues to slide in and out of me. Tears form in my eyes as I wait. The pleasure mixes with the pain of not being able to come. His fingers uncurl from mine and he captures my chin, pulling my face closer to his. He lowers his head and presses his lips hard against mine.

Trailing down to my ear, he continues to thrust into me. "Play now, my little dove," he whispers as he rolls his fingers around my nipple. I barely have to touch myself before everything is too much, and I crumble under him. His groan is entirely too sexy as he fills me, and I come again, hearing his voice in my ear. His breath on my neck is sensitive and sends goosebumps through my body.

"So fucking perfect." He pulls out and heads to the bathroom.

My head is swimming, and I just lay there in the afterglow's pleasure. He comes back with a washcloth, cleaning the sweat off my neck and forehead and wiping between my legs. "Get ready for bed. I'm exhausted," he says.

I make my way to the bathroom and pull on an oversized shirt, then go sit outside with him where we share a smoke.

My mind lingers on the subtle shift I observed afterwards. This time, he remained silent and didn't utter those three magical words. I wonder if he didn't really mean it the first time, it was just something that was said in the moment. My mind is great at picking apart a single thought until I feel nothing but hopelessness. I look towards him, and his eyes are on mine.

"Are you alright?"

I nod, dropping the cigarette in the ashtray. I go inside and get into bed.

He isn't far behind me, his body settling in next to mine. "I love you, Marla."

I say nothing. My chest tightens, and I fall into the darkness of sleep.

Fourteen

Sebastian

Weeks pass and, although I offer to take Marla everywhere that she needs to after the meeting with her sister, she says she doesn't need the help. An icy sheet of distance has fallen between us. I get a message here and there, but otherwise it's been pretty quiet. It drives me crazy with emotion. Night after night, I lurk outside her window or sneak into her apartment, listening to the haunting sound of her sobs.

Tonight, as I finish selling the drugs, I slip into her apartment to watch her sleep. Rage fills me, knowing she can sleep without me isn't something I can stand. Before I lose control of my emotions, I leave the apartment.

As I drive around, the neon lights of the city illuminate the faces of the women standing on the street corners. They stumble around, not knowing the danger they're in. I pull over, and help three of them into the car. My shoulders tighten. Tension courses through me, my nerves on edge, but without my dove's soothing presence, this is what I must do.

Upon arriving home, I corral them in the confines of the cages. I pace the floor of the shed, my hands running through my hair in frustration. The sound of crying and moaning fills the air as the bitches realize the extent of their containment. The feeling of being ignored ignites a raging fire within me. "I don't want to die." The blonde whimpers as I open the cage.

"Sorry sweetheart." I wrap my hand in her hair and drag her along the floor. After I've sliced her throat, the blood drains into the bucket. The screams of her friends serve as a chilling backdrop. The other two come to the same fate as the first. As I drain them all, the sounds of their fading breaths merge with the echoes of death, blood, and despair, creating an eerie symphony that brings me a fleeting sense of freedom. I stalk out to the backyard, feeling the rough texture of the shovel in my hands as I begin digging.

As I haul the women over my shoulder and into the hole, I realize nothing will ever fill the emptiness in my heart except for Marla. Without her, I'm nothing but a fucking monster, a danger to everyone. The soil shifts and blankets the shattered corpses, offering a feast for the maggots to consume. I walk back into the shed to clean up my mess, taking care with the buckets to feed the plants. These sacrifices were meaningless, failing to ease the intense anger inside me. Only her presence can bring solace.

Over the next few days, I throw myself into my work. With the access I have to the main supplier through the bar meetings, I'm able to reach a larger clientele and I'm not stuck with the run-down buildings. I still do them, but the cash flow that comes from the higher-quality clients is a bonus. Being the owner of Marla's building came with more work than I expected, so I've been interviewing and hiring a few maintenance people.

After not hearing from her for over a week, I sit in my car and watch her come out from the mental health centre. Marla walks out wearing dark, wide-legged jeans and a tight black tee with a long white sleeve under. Her hair is a mess again, bangs falling in her eyes. Her face holds no smile, and I know that she is just as unhappy without me.

Walking with a blonde girl, they go to a coffee shop close to the centre. I'm glad she has a friend, but the anger brews deep inside that she can function but isn't talking to me. I finish my deals in the building near hers and I stand outside her door, waiting for her.

"Sebastian, hey!" She seems surprised that I'm here. I've told her more than once how much she means to me and yet she is caught off guard that I'm standing here waiting for her.

"Marla, how are you doing?"

Her long-sleeved white shirt is too hot for the spring day, and it bothers me because I know she's hiding again. I'm angry at myself for not taking better care of her. I've been slacking on watching her, I haven't been here when she obviously needed me.

She holds open the door of the building and I follow her.

"I'm alright. Taking it day by day. It's just been hard. My mind has been really dark, and I didn't want to bother you with it."

Swiftly, I grab her wrist as she sets her purse down. I stare into her hazel eyes. "You are never a bother, you should know this by now."

Her gaze drops and so does my heart. I won't listen to the words she might say, the complications of our actions for killing her mother may be too high and I can't bear the thought of our relationship ending. Was it all too much for her? Am I too much for her? I can't possibly face a life without her in it, stalking her isn't enough anymore.

"Sorry. It's just been extremely hard. My siblings blame me for my mother's death. Not that they think I did it, but because I didn't break up with you sooner. The funeral was a shitshow. My uncle straight up accused me of killing his sister, and his cunt wife was hot on his heels to speak up."

She grabs a beer from the fridge and hands one to me. I didn't know she even drank, since she never has in the time I've been watching her.

"I'm sorry. They are blind to what they haven't experienced. They only speak from a place high on their horses. All of them will fall someday." I take a drink from my beer and watch her drink hers.

"Yeah, it's just been hard. I'm used to being blamed, but I never thought they would corral around me like this. No one from the family has reached out to me at all. They went through the will and apparently Ashley and Michael got the house, so I won't be burning it down."

"We still could, but I think it would look suspicious. They can live with the black karma and ghosts now."

I check my watch, knowing I have to go. "I can come back later if you'd like?" While I stand by the door, I look at her. My chest fills with love and dread pokes through my ribs.

"I'm going to go to bed after you leave. I'll see you soon, okay?" She stands on her tippy toes and kisses my cheek. Jasmine shampoo floods my senses and I want nothing more than to stay, but I have money to make and people to pay.

After collecting all the money and paying the supplier, I drive home with the random woman in the back of the car. I wanted to take someone from Marla's family, but that has to be her decision. The urges I have can't be curbed when I'm alone. They are just too strong. They wrap around the tendrils of my mind and the tension is too much to ignore without her.

After setting up the table, I pull out her teeth and listen to her screams and pleas for a little while before sliding the knife across her throat, ending the annoyance.

While I dig the hole in the yard, I think about how far Marla and I have gotten, from the times I spent watching her to having her as my own. But I feel like she's falling through my fingers. I don't want to crush her by gripping too hard, but I can't survive without her.

As I walk back into the shed, I clean off the tools. While I wait for the body to be empty of blood, I walk to the little room. I open the toolbox that holds rows of teeth, finding the best two and then I pull the metal wire down from the shelf and work at binding them. The work is tedious, but I know she loves oddities and this will make for a great pair of earrings. As I finish the intricate design, I heat the metals to make the part that will slide into her perfect ears. They look great, so I put them into a small box and walk it out to the tool bench.

I cross the room to pick up the woman. She isn't overly large, but I seem to be out of shape from not doing this as often. I'm breathless when I reach the hole. The other night when I killed, my strength must have came from adrenaline. After dumping her in and filling it back up, I pat the ground so it's even.

Once I'm back in the shed, I clean everything up. Grabbing the pail of blood, I work at feeding all the plants in the backyard. The different colours of blooms are really coming to life and the essence of those lost are living through the beauty of this lavish garden.

I rinse the pail, grab the gift box, and head into the house. I shower the night off of me, the dirt and grime swirling down the drain.

Marla consumes my mind. If the situation demands it, I'll monitor her again. I lay in bed, my mind racing with thoughts and worries, unable to shut it off and fall asleep. Something is wrong. I can feel it within my bones. My heart hurts and I know Marla is in trouble.

Without dwelling on it, I slip on jeans and a t-shirt, grab my keys and I'm out the door driving into town. Being on the outskirts has its perks, like the freedom to do whatever I want in my yard, but being so far from Marla isn't great. As I get to her apartment, most of the lights are off except for her bedroom and I think about entering through the window, but the streets are busier than they ever have been. I walk back to the car and get the keys for the building. Entering through the back and finding her apartment, I stand outside her door for a few minutes, deciding what is right and what is wrong.

Throwing away my moral compass, I unlock her door and walk inside. Soft music fills the air, and as I make my way to her bedroom, I hope I'm not too late.

She's sits on her bed. There are already three perfectly lined cuts on her upper arm. The blood beads and then trickles down her delicate skin, and I watch her hold the blade and look down at her arms. She pauses as I pass the entranceway to her bedroom, and I hate how life has bent her to be her own worst enemy.

"How did you know I needed you?"

"I don't know. My heart told me you were in trouble. Are you?" I walk to her and pull the blade from her hand. I lick my finger and run it over the lines on her arm, bringing it back to my lips, tasting her salty metallic essence. It's too soon for her to do this. It's not her time.

"Maybe, but self-harm isn't suicide."

I don't answer as I walk to the bathroom to pull a washcloth off the shelf and wet it to clean her up. "I know it isn't. It's a coping mechanism to hold the demons back. It makes the numb feeling of despair slow down and gives you a feeling of happiness that no one can understand. But you will never be able to cut deep enough to reach the euphoria you once did, you will always be chasing a ghost," I tell her as I work on her wounds.

"I feel lost," she whispers.

Looking around her room, I spot a large bag and instinctively start sifting through her clothes, picking out the ones she wears the most. As I hand her a hoodie and wait for her to put it on, she asks, "Where are we going?"

"Home. You aren't lost. I've found you. I'll always find you. Doesn't matter what happens, I will always find you." I sling her bag over my shoulder and hold out my other hand. Marla takes it and starts walking to the door.

"How did you get in here?" she asks as she slips on her shoes.

"Door was unlocked."

We walk to the car and get in. She doesn't say much as we drive and as I pull into the driveway, I wait for her to get out. "Thank you. I know that I've been awful lately. It's just been really hard."

"No need to thank me. You can stay here as long as you want. Loving someone means you love the good parts and also the shitty parts. Every broken piece of a person is loveable if you are with the right person."

Marla puts her hand in mine and we walk away from the car. "I love you too. I know I don't say it much, but I just didn't know how much to say it."

"You can say it as much or as little as you need to. I'll still come, even if you don't love me anymore," I tell her.

"How did I get so lucky to find such an amazing guy?" I smirk in the dark as we reach the house and I unlock the door. "I ask myself every day how I was chosen to receive your love."

She kisses me as we get through the entranceway. My fingers tangle in her hair, allowing me to pull her closer as our kiss intensifies. I pull away from her as I flick on the kitchen light. "You are free here, my dove. It's not much, but it's home."

I show her the living room, and the front porch, and we walk upstairs to the bedrooms and bathroom. There is a tiny balcony off my bedroom, a guest room, and a bathroom with an ancient tub. She looks over everything before looking back at me.

"Can we go to sleep?" she questions.

I can only smile as I finally have my Marla in my bedroom. As soon as I lay down, my dreams pull me under and I'm content.

Fifteen

Marla

I lay next to Sebastian. My mind races from thought to thought and I can't relax enough to fall asleep. I slowly wiggle out of his grasp. His chest rises and falls so little, I wonder if he's even breathing. I take his sweater and pull it over my shoulders, letting myself out onto the balcony. The view is gorgeous. Although it's dark, much darker than anywhere in the city, the moon shines down, illuminating his vast garden. I would have never guessed that he had such a big green thumb, but the backyard is like an enchanted oasis of blooms and landscape—all he's missing is a waterfall of some sort.

I'm almost positive I locked the door. Everything before the cutting is fuzzy. It's like life is wiped from my mind when I think of the release that will come. Nobody really knows the pain that invades my mind and seeps into my heart. I'm able to put on the show. The curtain opens for the day with people, and I can fake that I'm alright, that I'll be fine. But the pain never ceases. It eats at the edges of my heart, slows the heartbeat so only blackness beats through my veins until I'm home and can cut it out, slice to make sure I still bleed red, and the darkness hasn't taken everything from me. The crimson droplets are so pretty, making me feel better. It mimics the way drugs once felt, but I don't risk everything for the warm fuzzy feeling. The pain flows out freely as I add more lines to my collection.

When I'm with Sebastian, the pain isn't as strong. It feels more like a paper cut than the gash across my heart.

My fingers delve into his pocket and emerge with a cigarette and a lighter, its metallic surface glinting in the light. As I inhale the smoke, I feel the cool night air on my skin, and I exhale slowly, looking up at the full moon in the sky.

I had thought that killing my mother would bring me peace, but the opposite is true. Every time I go for mental help, I wait anxiously, afraid that each passing day will be the one where they declare me an unfit member of society. I'll get the mark and that will be the end. If I'm going to die, it'll be at my own hand. I never want to go out in a white, sterile room with chemical smells and uncaring people.

"Marla, my dove. What are you doing out here?"

I turn to look at him. His looks are edgy, but he is still so beautiful to me that sometimes it's painful that he cares about me. He settles beside me, his face is creased by the pillow, his naked upper body shows me the artwork covering all his hard muscles, his angled sharp jaw covered in shadowed stubble. I drag my eyes from his lip ring to his dark brown eyes. His hair is messy and hangs over his forehead. I hand him a cigarette.

"Couldn't sleep. My mind is too busy. I didn't know you were such a green thumb. The gardens are beautiful, but you need a waterfall."

His fingers touch mine lightly. I bring my knees up to lean on them. He puts his elbows on his knees and leans forward as he blows out smoke. "I can do that. Never wanted a waterfall, but if you do, then it's done."

"Why will you do anything I ask?"

"Because you are the light at the end of my tunnel, you bring me hope for a better life, that maybe, just maybe, love can conquer our darkest moments, that all the shit we go through has a purpose."

I think about it for a few minutes. "I'm the last person who should inspire hope and light. Is that the reason for the nickname?"

He chuckles softly, "Yeah. Seems lame, I know, but I ran over a list of normal nicknames and nothing suited you."

"You should think of me as a wren instead," I tell him.

"I'm not going to call you a wren." His face contorts, and I laugh.

"It's a symbol of both life and death across the world." I turn my head to gauge his reaction.

He shakes his head. "Still not going to call you my little wren, but I do vow to love you in life and in death. No matter what happens, I promise to find you in the next life and love you with the same intensity that I do now."

I smirk. Hope is a terrible feeling, and it swells in my chest, threatening to break my ribs because his mouth tells me such beautiful lies. I'm not worthy of that much love. My eyes burn, and a yawn escapes me.

"Now, can we go to bed?"

I nod. "I'm sorry for keeping you up."

He slaps my ass as I crawl back through the window. "You don't get to keep saying sorry. I don't know if it's the Canadian ingrained in you, but I don't need your apologies."

As we lay in bed, I look in his direction. "The pain didn't go away after she was gone." His fingertips crawl over my shoulder, dancing their way down the column of my neck.

"I know. It did at first, though, right?"

"Yeah, when we first did it, that night I felt high. It was exhilarating. The drop-off was steep, and I should have anticipated it. It's not like I could talk about it with anyone. No one is going to understand that I killed my mother and fuck, did it feel good. I'm still glad she's dead but my pain is still on the surface, just under the layer of my skin." His fingers find their way to my hair, playing with the strands which makes me relax next to him.

"I have to cut your hair again. We can do that tomorrow. I bought you something, but I left it downstairs. Remind me. Marla I know the pain is still grasping you. The demons grip you. But patience is my style, it's kinda my thing, they don't understand that I'll hold on to you tighter, that I'll do whatever it takes to rip you from their claws."

I move closer to him, my head pressed into his chest. His manly citrus cologne fills my nose and he rests his head on mine. "I hope you keep me from them. My soul needs peace, but if it can't have that, I'll settle for whatever I can enjoy here on earth."

We sit at his kitchen table. The chairs are old but sturdy. The wallpaper is faded on the walls, some parts are peeling. "Did you get your father's house and never decide to decorate?"

He looks around, the trim around the doors is scratched up, the floors are linoleum and the colours in each room are vintage as hell. "Pretty much. Does it look like I know how to decorate?"

"Your tattoos all fit. Just figured you'd be fantastic at decorating." His face breaks into a huge smile.

"I can plan a tattoo. I can plan a garden, but give me a room, and ask me what colour curtains go with the wallpaper? Not a clue." He leaves for a minute and comes back with a towel, a comb, and scissors.

"My salon is open again. Although I don't have a brush, apparently." His brows pinch together. He shakes his head and puts the towel around my shoulders. "The usual?" I can only laugh.

"You look like this tough grunge-style dude, and yet you are so lame you make me laugh."

"Isn't that why you keep me around? For the laughs?"

I hold the towel around myself and smile. "Yeah, something like that."

When he's finished, I go for a shower in his incredibly old bathroom. The tub has claws and at one point was probably gorgeous, but now it's worn and chipped. The shower curtain goes all the way around the tub and the water pressure isn't as strong as in my apartment, but it's good enough for now. When I get to his room, heated from the shower, get dressed in capri pants and a long sweater and comb my hair out with my fingers.

"Here, I got these from that oddity shop." Sebastian startles me, but I turn and grab the box. I pull off the lid and find a pair of earrings. They are made from teeth, canines at some point. The metal design above them is gorgeous.

"These are breathtaking. Thank you so much." I put them in my ears, crossing the room to the dresser with a mirror, and look at them. The silver catches the light, and I can't believe he got these. "They must have been expensive?" He shrugs his shoulder.

"Since you don't have to go to the mental health centre today, what did you want to do?"

"I want to know if we kill the rest of the family if I'll feel better? Will it help?" He looks at me, and a slow smile creeps across his face.

"It might, but it might not. It's hard to say, the high might only last for a few days and I don't want you to crash again. I can't handle the loss of you."

I walk to the doorway where he stands and run my hands under his t-shirt to the hard muscles underneath." They didn't save me. They think it's all my fault."

His hand cups my jaw and he runs his thumb over my cheek. "It still stands. You could have the high and pull away from me. I'm selfish, Marla, I can't help it."

I inch closer, nipping his jaw with my teeth. The burning lust in his eyes makes me confident. "I won't. I'm yours."

"We'll see about that." His hand moves from my jaw to my neck, and he pins me against the door frame. "I have something to show you. If you decide you are still mine after you see the real me? Then I'll kill anyone you want. I'll hold them down so you can carve them into shreds."

The brattiness fades but desire fills me. "Deal."

He arches his eyebrow as his hand pulls away from my throat and trails down my body to grasp my hand. We walk down the stairs and out of the house, then stand in the backyard surrounded by the gardens. The hydrangeas are stunning. The way the flowers bloom, the colours that decorate the entire backyard, leave me in wonderment. I don't know what he could show me that would make me want to run away and leave him.

Sixteen

Sebastian

Her eyes scan over the backyard. She adores the flowers and I wonder if she would love them as much if she knew what was under them. I hold her hand and pull her along the path further into the yard. The large shed blends with the trees, camouflaged nicely by the overgrowth I've never cleared.

"What's in there?" she asks, her eyes piqued with interest. Her pert nose might be one of my favourite features on her face.

"Let's see." I know I'm risking everything–every hour I've spent watching her, every plan I've put in place, but I don't see how we can continue our relationship if she doesn't know who I really am.

Her hand trails along the rough stone wall for support as we make our way through the door, and she recoils at the touch of sticky cobwebs. With a creaking sound, I pull open the plastic panels and the musty smell of the room hits me as I step inside and flick on the light. Despite her stillness, her eyes dart around the room, taking everything in. Her gaze lingers on the crates, the table and the restraints leaning against the wall.

"Who are you?" Her voice quivers slightly, but her eyes remain the same, and she's not running out the door.

"I take care of people." My dove walks further into the room, her hand delicately running over the metal cages used for keeping people. She does a full circle of the room.

"What's in there?" she points to the red door.

"Tools," I reply.

"Alright, so are you going to cut me into little pieces and feed me to your garden, or am I safe?"

When I hear her odd question, my brow furrows and I cock my head. "I'd never hurt you. I couldn't even if I wanted to because it would hurt me far worse."

She purses her lips, clicks her tongue, and runs her hand over the red door. "Show me."

Shock fills me. I thought she'd run away, beg me to take her back to her apartment, or at least be angry. I never thought she'd be this interested, and it shows me we are meant to be together.

I unlock the door and stand outside of it. She enters and looks over the tools in the small room. Her eyes sweep the space. Without touching anything, she leaves the room and comes to stand next to me. "This is where you'd help kill the family?"

"Yeah. I thought it would be less suspicious if they just disappeared over time, rather than everyone suddenly dropping dead in their houses."

She walks over to the table, looking over the angle of it and the drains underneath. "What do you do here?"

"I drain the blood of the person. The essence that they have within them helps my gardens grow better."

A smile ghosts her lips. "The restraints?"

I walk closer to her. "Sometimes people need to exhaust themselves before I can help them." Her fingers slide over the metal, the chains and she looks back at me.

"I still love you. I'm not running anywhere."

"Is it only because you want me to kill your family?"

"Nah, I'll be there to help." I stand behind her and pull her to me.

"Now I just feel like you might be using me." I run my hand through her hair. Taking a fistful, I pull her head back to my shoulder and I run my tongue over the length of her neck. "Show me, prove to me how much you are mine."

"Wanna tie me up? Restrain me and show me who's the boss?" She arches an eyebrow and bites her lip.

"No, I'm going to make you beg me to mark you." I let go of her and head into the small room, grabbing an unused knife and my favourite large blade, and I walk out with it to find her leaning against the tool bench. It's lower than most workbenches, but has served its purpose for me. I look forward to fucking her in the same place I've taken many lives.

I lay the knives down on the wood top. Lowering my head, I catch her lips with mine, lightly at first, before I deepen the kiss. I pull away from her perfect mouth, running my tongue over her lip. "Do you trust me?" I ask.

"Yes."

That's all I need. I remove the sweater from her body and pull the capris off, so she's standing with only panties on in front of me. She shivers and her nipples harden. Bringing my mouth to her nipple, I suck on the flesh and swirl my tongue around the hard point. My hands grip her hips and I pick her up, placing her on top of the wooden bench. She gasps, and I hold her by her neck, pushing her down flat.

My hands run over her smooth skin, hooking her legs over my shoulders as I look down at her. My perfect sweet Marla, ready to prove her love to me, ready to show me she is truly mine. I grasp my favourite knife, the one I've used to give people the sweet kiss of death. I trail the tip of the blade over her skin. The cold metal makes her quiver as I cut her panties from her body, and her breath hitches. "You are so fucking perfect, you were made for me."

With knife in hand, I move my head down, keeping her legs on my shoulders. I inhale her sweet scent, surprised that I can see her slit glisten. She's turned on by this, which makes me harder than I've been in a very long time. I place my tongue on her, tasting her and exploring her wetness slowly, my tongue sweeping over her clit. She tenses, but I pull away. She isn't going to come until she's marked with my initials.

I put down that knife and pick up the new one, drawing a line down the centre of her, running the tip over the skin between her tits. As it lowers, she tries to clench her thighs tighter, looking for any friction she can find. I hang onto the blade and slide the handle over her slit. She cries out as I tease her with the cold metal. I slide it into her wetness, and slowly, I fuck her with the handle. Mixing the things I love together makes me drunk with lust.

She whimpers as I pull it out of her. "Please, can I come?" She begs me like the good fucking girl she is.

"No, my dove, what should you beg for? To prove to me how much you love me?"

"Mark me, I'll be yours for eternity. Forever." Marla's chest quickens with the breaths she takes. The words are music to my ears. She lets out a soft sigh as I lower her legs from my shoulders and turn her on the wooden top. I hastily discard my shirt and climb onto the table, positioning myself with one knee beside her and the other wedged between her legs. I watch her hips grind against my jeans, her heat soaking me.

Above her heart, I etch an S in her skin. The blood beads and flows over her perfect flesh. I move closer and my tongue swipes over my work. Her back arches under me and I continue with the Y, my initials carved into her forever. Her essence is now a part that will live in me for the end of time. I continue to clean her.

I pull my knee away and play with her until she explodes over my hand.

"Yes, fuck yes."

"Mine, forever."

"Yours. But what about me? You aren't mine." She pouts, her hooded eyes drunk with blood and lust.

I lean back on my heels. I didn't think about this part. I never thought she would want to mark me. As I lay down, the roughness of the wood catches me off guard, but I splay my legs around Marla. She gets up and crawls over me, grabbing the knife as she straddles me. A mixture of fear and anticipation runs through me. She lowers her mouth to mine, kissing me, her tongue intertwining with mine before she pulls back. Blood runs down over her chest and I bring my fingers up to wipe it away, but she pushes my hand away.

She runs the blade over me the same way I did to her. The hard metal runs endorphins through me at a fast pace. My dick is impossibly hard. She examines my chest, looking for a piece of empty skin. There isn't a lot, but she finds the untouched tiny piece over my heart. The prick of the tip of the knife turns into a sting as she drags the blade down, breaking the skin. She doesn't stop until she's done.

"M.L.," she breathes before lowering her face to my chest. Her tongue dances over my skin, cleaning my blood off and trailing to my neck, tasting me everywhere. "Mine," she breathes into my ear before trailing my jaw with kisses. I reach up and hold her hips as she rolls them onto my hardness. Marla leans back to undo my belt, unzipping my jeans. She rips them down and my cock slaps against my stomach.

"Fuck me, Marla. I'm yours." As her eyes burn into mine, she moves slightly and I can feel her heat over the head of my dick. Slowly, inch by inch, she moves down, taking my full hard cock inside of her tight, perfect cunt. She rides me. After a few minutes, she leans down into the crook of my neck. I place one hand on her hip and fuck up into her as hard as I can. "Fuck yes, come all over my cock." Her walls clench over me and wetness gushes as she comes.

"Get up," I whisper. She does exactly what I say. When she is standing, I place my hand on the back of her neck, holding her down against the workbench. I hook one of her legs up with my hand so I can fuck her. As I hold her as tight as I can, she crumbles under me, coming undone as I thrust into her. My orgasm quickly approaches, and I pull out.

Lifting my grip on her neck, I push her to her knees. I stroke my dick over her face, and watch as her pouty lips open. I jerk myself harder as I fill her mouth with ropes of my come.

My hand finds the workbench to hold on to. The room spins slightly as I breathe. I hold out my hand, and when she takes it, I pull her up to me, wrapping my arms around her as I kiss her.

"I love you," I say as I pick up her clothes and hand them to her. I do up my pants and move the knives to the small room to clean up.

"I love you, Sebastian." The amount of love I have for her would alarm her, but everything I've ever wanted with her is falling into place, just like I knew it would.

Seventeen

Cavum Terra

"Berimund, things are worse." I look at Giso and roll my eyes, the knowledge is nothing new for me. I knew before we started implementing these new ideas that it would be a terrible thing.

"What have you tried?"

"We've briefed the souls, they don't generally believe us. When they do believe us, things get chaotic," Tanca says.

As I walk to the edge of our land, I look over the property. Shadow demons run wildly through the red and orange haze. Fear is in the air, and when I look further into the bare trees, the branches are grotesque and sharp, darkness envelopes everything. Just as I had suspected, it would make everything worse if we gave the new souls a briefing. Telling someone who killed themselves that they now belong in a world where they can never outrun the demons from their minds, the things that have tormented them for their entire existence on Earth will now rip them to shreds forever. The others are idiots to think that this knowledge would have been powerful.

"The darkness has turned into blackness. It seeps through the forests and the entire realm is filled with fear. The chaos is too much. You were right from the start." Giso sighs as she walks to the edge with me.

"What about the demons?" I know we had played with the idea over the last couple of decades to have conversations with them as they arrived. I needed them to stop hurting the souls to near death. Killing them here defeats the purpose of the realm.

"They don't care. Their newfound power is far too great to give a shit about the souls they have haunted for so many years. Each demon I've had a conversation with shared the goal of the realm—to torture for eternity—but they aren't understanding how killing the souls will zap them out of existence. They listen, but they disregard the message as soon as they feel the power they hold. It was all for nothing." Giso bows her head.

"The darkness is too much. It lasts much longer now, the smell of fear seeps into our houses, and the rage burns my eyes. Every emotion is magnified and creeps into every available opening. It's too much," Tanca says.

"As I suspected. Immediately, we will stop conversing with the demons. Let them have the power, they won't change. The souls, we will only tell them if they seek us out, a few answers, but enough that they can figure it out quickly." I tell everyone as I walk back to my house.

Opening the main door I look at the manifesto. No souls are scheduled for at least a decade. Time moves differently here compared to Earth, everything is slower and lasts much longer. What I can do is provide bite-size pieces of information for those who will be coming in.

"What about the souls who get hurt? We need to fix that issue," Tanca asks.

I straighten my robe and close the book.

When I face them, I decide we will cast a powerful spell over each soul to enter Cavum Terra. "When each soul arrives, we will bless them with the resilience needed to survive, with the ability to heal after the demons have taken them to the brink of existence. Thus making them durable enough to withstand the torture for eternity.

"It seems like the best idea. The current souls won't make it, but for the next it will be a must."

I nod at the words. It's the best we can do and might cut down on the emotions we have to endure.

Fear, anger, and anguish are the highest on the list to emote harmful toxins our way.

"I'll see you when the next batch comes in," I tell them as I disappear into my quarters. The wooden bedframe in the corner of the room is intricately designed, the mattress firm but comfortable, and I've exhausted myself from the day. Until I'm needed again I will be in slumber.

Eighteen

Marla

The cuts on my skin sting in the shower. I'm getting ready to go to the mental health centre. I don't want another fine, or to be taken away. I didn't think giving a blade to Sebastian during sex would be so incredibly hot. It lit every nerve ending in my body on fire. Afterwards, the way he held me close, was everything I was missing from my drops when I cut alone.

"Hurry. Do you want coffee?" he asks me as he turns on the tap to brush his teeth. The water turns ice cold in the shower, and I twist off the water.

"Happy to see me?" he asks as his eyes trail over my hardened nipples. I roll my eyes and towel off.

"Stay. I'm going to cover your initials." He returns with a tube of cream and a bandage. I notice his chest has a similar bandage.

"Won't you get a fine for not coming today?"

"No. I'll be out to get your aunt and uncle. These are the directions you said?" he opens his phone and shows me what I told him last night.

I nod. "Why won't you get a fine for not coming to the centre today?"

He sighs and his warm fingers grip my chin tightly. "Because I'm not registered or mandated to attend. I saw you one day when I was passing by and knew I wanted to meet you, so I pretended."

I push out of his grip, hanging the towel on the hook. I make my way to the bedroom to get dressed. "You lied to me," I say as he stands in the doorway. I fasten my bra on and slip a long sleeve shirt over my head before pulling on red panties, and hear his breath suck in.

"Technically, I never lied. I do indeed have anger problems. Experts would probably love for me to be going if they knew."

I grab my jeans and slide them on, fastening my belt. I slip past him again to brush out my hair, then add a layer of red lip stain and mascara. As I try to push past him again, he doesn't move.

His hand circles my throat and he presses me against the wall. "I didn't lie, Marla. I failed to elaborate, but I didn't lie."

"So, you pretended to be suffering like the rest of us just to be with me?" I look into his eyes. His grip on me doesn't lessen as he presses his lips to mine when he pulls away his gaze intensely watches me.

"Yes, exactly that. I told you I was selfish, and I wanted you." I digest his words. It's crazy he went to these lengths to be near me.

On one hand, I should be mad that he lied, but technically, he didn't even lie. I think back to our conversations in the early days, and he never said they mandated him like they did me. He just answered my questions and didn't expand. Sebastian went to those lengths to see me, and hang out all day in the depressing centre just to get to know me. I know you can go to prison for being there if you don't have to be. He risked everything just to be with me. My stomach jumps and my heart swells. The tears prick my eyes before I can stop them.

"You're right. You didn't lie, but I'd appreciate no more secrets like that again." I bring my hand up to his face to clear the hair from his eyes. He should cut his hair soon, although I love the longer length.

"I bared everything to you last night–everything that I am, that I like and what I've done." My mouth curls into a smile.

"Did you say there was coffee?"

He lowers his head and kisses me before turning away and wrapping his hand in mine. "Yes, let's get you fed and caffeinated for your fun day at the centre. I'll go capture your aunt and uncle and have them ready, waiting for you."

"Can we do tacos for dinner?" I ask, hope blooming in my chest. I know I'll have to go home to my apartment eventually, but I'll live this game of house for as long as I can.

"Of course. After everything is done. I'll dig the hole while I wait for your day to be finished. I think we have to grab a few things from your apartment if you want to keep staying here."

"Dig a hole? And I'll have to go home soon. My landlord hates when people stay away too long." I grasp the warm mug with my hands and take a sip. He hands me a plate of toast with peanut butter on it.

"Your landlord won't care, but we can get your laptop and stuff if you want it."

"Peter is an asshole. He will start harassing me if I stay away too long. He's not like most landlords, he's obsessive and creepy."

A snort escapes Sebastian and I pinch my eyebrows when I look at him. "It's not funny."

He sits across from me at the table with his own toast and coffee. "I know it's not funny, he was obsessive and creepy. But he's also taken the long dirt nap, so when I tell you he won't care, trust me, he isn't going to care."

It dawns on me that he's killed Peter. That's why I've had so much peace in the last while—because he's gone. I haven't heard from the new landlords, but the building has improved in cleanliness and things are getting fixed quicker. "Why did you kill him? and why the hole?"

He sighs, setting his toast down. He looks at me and takes a long pull from his mug. "Because he was a creepy bastard to you. That night I got lost, I saw him trying to muscle his way into your apartment and he touched you. The way he talked to you that night? Fuck that."

All these things he's done for me, that I had no idea were even happening. My love for him surrounds me. It's overwhelming and not enough all at the same time.

"The hole is for your dearest aunt and uncle. We'll have to go out and buy more flowers tomorrow. I'll even let you pick the colours." He picks up his toast and finishes eating.

"The flowers all have people under them?" He presses his lips into a thin line and nods.

"Ready? Or do you have more questions?"

"I'm ready. What are your favourite colours for the gardens?" I ask.

He shakes his head with a small smile on his lips. "Just a variety. I've never really thought about favourites."

After a depressing day at the centre, I wait for Sebastian outside, leaning against the white stone wall. "Can I bum a smoke from you?" Jess asks as she leaves the centre's door.

"These things will kill ya."

She laughs. "One day." She lights the smoke, and we exhale together.

"What a shit day. I really was so close to the number, and they just like to crush all the hope you have." I think about her words, and I realize she's probably right. They give you an inch of hope and crush every single shred to heal into smithereens.

"I'll see you next time. Don't do anything stupid," I whisper. I like her, and I'd like to hang out more, but currently my life is taking on a fresh adventure.

On the way to my apartment, I think about the next steps we will take. My aunt and uncle have never believed a word out of my mouth. They sit atop their high horses, and it will be a thing of beauty to watch them fall. I'm almost excited. Everyone who turned a blind eye, every single one of them who could have saved me, will pay for what they didn't choose to do.

"I told you to meet me at the park. Get in." I hear Sebastian's voice from the road. He's slowly driving along and pulls over so I can get in.

"I'm sorry." I don't recall him saying to meet him at the park, but my thoughts have been in one big fog lately.

"No, you don't have to be sorry. Let's go have some fun." As we drive home, excitement runs through me, but my nerves make me shake. I can't sit still and fidget with my hair, and my fingernails, and eventually let out a deep sigh.

"I can do it all. You say your piece and leave, and I'll finish the job."

I know he would do that for me. He would burn the world down if I asked him to, but I feel like this is what I have to do. "I think I want to do it. Honestly, I need to do it."

Sebastian doesn't say a word, just turns up the metal band playing on the radio, and I zone out to the music until we're pulling into the driveway.

"They aren't happy, I mean obviously not, but they turned feral."

I giggle thinking about it being any other way.

We walk to the shed and down the stairs, the cobwebs that cover the entranceway are annoying, but as we pass the plastic panels, I see both my Aunt Janet and Uncle Donald crouching in the crates. The air smells like urine, and as I get closer, I see the puddles under them on the metal crate bottoms. Perspiration runs down both their faces.

"Marla, thank god you are here. You need to save us. A fucking psychopath took us today from our house," Janet pleads. Her shrill voice throttles my eardrums. With a slight tilt of my head, I cast my eyes upon them. My maniacal laughter echoes through the room. "He's not a psychopath, he's my boyfriend."

Her eyes widen, and my uncle doesn't even look up. It's like he has accepted his fate. He knows he didn't save me. "What do you mean?" Janet mumbles.

"Remember the parties you used to come to at Mother's house? The nights you would drink and play games and laugh at me? Remember how you told me I'd grow up and amount to nothing? Or better yet, what about the times when you told me I deserved every abusive thing that happened to me?"

"It wasn't like that, Marla. It wasn't that big of a deal. You take things out of context, you don't use your brain to think properly. I've only tried to guide you, do what's best for you. You know this." A cackle escapes before I can control it.

"Janet, shut the fuck up. You're not making anything better." Good ole Uncle Don.

"You've accepted what you've done, haven't you?" I direct my attention to him. He doesn't look up at me and just nods.

"Pathetic. I'm your fucking wife. You are such a pathetic, weak coward."

I walk over to Sebastian, who's standing by the workbench. I pick up the knife that he has laid on the worktop. "The hole is done, the table is set up, it's up to you how you want to do this. I don't want to take anything away from your experience."

"I don't know how to set up the table. I'm sure they have great nutrients in their blood for the gardens. They only eat organic shit."

He laughs. I don't know why, but he continues to chuckle as he hooks up the bucket and drains. "Why are you laughing?"

"Because most people in the backyard were drug addicts, the blood has done its job, even though the humans it came from weren't great."

I smile, opening the crate for my Uncle Don. "If you give me trouble, I slit your throat before we get to the table." He only nods as he walks meekly to the table. He lays down on the top without question. I've never seen someone so compliant. I almost feel bad, but he had just as much voice as anyone else and could have told them to stop abusing me. He could have been my saviour, but was only a servant.

"If you cut along here, the blood runs out, and gravity takes its own course. It needs pressure to hit the carotid artery. It'll be quick. He will be gone in minutes, unlike your mother."

Uncle Don's eyes widen when he realizes I'm the one who ended her, which is when he starts to struggle. Sebastian latches the straps down on Don's limbs. I look down at him, the man who could have shown me what real love was but chose not to, and I press the blade down into his neck. The skin gives way as the blade is applied harder. The blood runs in rivulets down his neck, staining his shirt and pooling on the table. I watch it rush out quicker, and it fascinates me. "Now, the only thing to do is to let him bleed out and for her to run out of steam."

"So, we just wait here listening to it? Breathing in piss, shit, and blood?" It doesn't go unnoticed that she's screaming even though she's shit her pants.

"We could go get tacos." He shrugs one shoulder, and I think about it for a minute, looking down at my clothes and seeing I'm still clean. I put the knife on the workbench and look at him.

"Are we going?"

"We have to make sure he's actually dead. We can't leave and have him spring to life and save her. Sorry, my dove, there are some rules." He walks over to the table and puts his fingers against my uncle's neck. "Soon."

Without a word, he leaves for the red room. He's gone for a few minutes before he locks it back up, handing me a heavy black apron. "For her, when we get back. It helps save your clothes. You don't notice it after a while."

Sebastian rechecks Don's pulse and nods his head. Grabbing his hat, he puts it on backwards and flicks off the light before holding open the plastic panels for me. They remind me of a grocery store or a butcher—both terrifying. You could get caught up in them, and a new fear would be unlocked.

"You can't just fucking leave me here. I told you that you would grow up to be nothing, and I was right. You're just a self-centred bitch."

I laugh. "And you are just a presumptuous cunt who shit her pants." I follow Sebastian out to the fresh air, gulping in as much as possible. My breathing increases, and the world tilts around me.

Nineteen

Sebastian

"Breathe in through your nose and out through your mouth, otherwise you are going to go into a panic," I tell her. Watching her gulp in the fresh air makes me remember my early days. "Breathe in slowly." I take a deep breath through my nose, and she mimics me. "Breathe it out slowly." We exhale together. She does it a few more times. "At first, it's hard. The smells are overwhelming, but eventually, it doesn't bother you anymore."

"When did it stop bothering you?"

I think about it as we walk to the car. Once we're in, I put my hand on her headrest and look over my shoulder to back out of the driveway. "After my father. He was a mean, sick motherfucker, but killing family is harder. With strangers, it's easier."

Driving to town, I go toward her apartment so she can pick up her laptop and anything else she might like.

"As for the smell, it dwindled away until one day, I didn't even notice it. But I have a weird thing about the floor. I hate when they piss or shit on it or, even worse, if I have to kill or hurt them before the table. I just hate when the floor is stained."

"Did you used to get in trouble when you spilled on the floor?"

I think about it as I parallel park, letting my mind scan through my memories. "Yeah, actually, I think so. I can't really remember. My father probably tried his best being the only one raising me, but he was a spiteful old bastard."

"It makes sense. I hate cleaning. Remember my mother told you I can't look after myself? I can. I just hate cleaning. Growing up, I would always do my best to help her and clean around the house, but it was never good enough. It didn't matter how hard I tried, they always saw it as the worst job ever. Now I hate it."

I turn the car off and nod. "It makes sense. I wish I could have found you sooner, because I would have saved you years ago."

As we leave the car, I circle to Marla's side and she takes my hand as we walk into her apartment.

"I wish we could have met sooner, too."

"I just have to grab my laptop so I can try to work on some things for my clients." I walk towards the back porch.

"There's no reason to rush. Take your time." I've kept tabs on her apartment, and I know everything has been going as it should. While I sit out back, I light a cigarette and pull out my phone to put in our order for tacos. We should probably try new food.

She comes out and lights a smoke. "I wonder who the new landlord is. They are doing a much better job. I can't believe how clean the building is. They even fixed my sink, which has been broken for like a year."

Not saying anything, I just watch her. Her dark hair falls perfectly on her shoulders. I love the way her face gets animated as she talks about things that are important to her. I've fallen so fucking hard. I knew for a long time I desired her to be mine, but I had no idea that I would give the air in my lungs if she wanted me to.

"Are you even listening?" I crack a smile and bite my bottom lip, and she groans. "Fine, whatever."

"Your beauty, which sounds incredibly cheesy, distracted me. How many dates do you think we've had?"

She squints her eyes and curls her lips in a *'what the fuck is wrong with your brain'* kinda way. "What?"

"Just wondered if we were coming up to our fifth date. You know what that is, right?" A smirk forms.

"You are a doofus," she laughs and stubs out her cigarette.

"A marriage proposal. You promised, fifth date," I tell her, and we laugh as we walk through the apartment. She locks up, and we head to the car to pick up the taco order.

"It wasn't a promise. We never even shook on it." I pout as I get into the car and drive to the restaurant.

"If someone was going to put a ring on your finger, what kind of ring would you want?" I already know what I want to make. It's another oddity to find, or so I'll probably tell her. I have the tooth picked out. I've sealed it in epoxy resin so it will withstand chips and damage. The metal has been harder to form than the earrings were, but I think after a few more weeks I'll be able to figure it out.

"One of a kind, obviously," she says as we reach the taco place.

I smile as she gets out of the car to grab our order. I don't know if eating before killing is the right move for her, but I don't want her to pass out, and I know that afterward, the high is sometimes too much to want to eat.

"Can we eat by the water before we go back?" she asks. "It's depressing there, but I love the water. It always helps me."

I drive to the lake. The park has long been abandoned since the decay of the city has become worse. We get out of the car, walk to a rickety picnic table, and sit on top of it as we open our dinner

"You ordered burritos?" She asks as she unwraps hers. "Yeah, I thought we should branch out. Maybe next time we can even get pizza."

She rolls her eyes, inching closer to me so our shoulders are touching, and eats her food. While I look out over the water, I listen to her eat. "Well, what's the verdict? Can we add a new menu item?"

"Yeah, it's better than I thought it would be, and I guess trying new foods won't kill me," Marla says.

We stand and I grab her wrapper, and her hand with my other hand. "Ready to do this?" I ask, tossing out our garbage.

"As ready as I can be."

"You know, I'll do it all for you."

She nods as we reach the car. "I know. I can say what I have to get off my chest and you'll do the dirty work. But I need this. Being with you makes me happier. I don't feel as cloaked by the demons wrestling in my head, but this adds something I can't describe." The feelings are indescribable. No words can express how it feels to take away the life of someone who has hurt you deeply.

"I know." We drive home, quickly walk into the shed, and I pick up the full bucket. The aunt has quieted down, and deescalated to tears and whimpers. I walk back out to pour the blood over the soil to feed the flowers.

"How do you move the body?" she asks, looking at the man on the table and back at me.

I crack my neck, remove the restraints and pull him off the table, lifting under his arms and pulling him up the stairs to the hole in the backyard. His body lands with a thud. Marla stands at the edge and looks into the hole. "Guess that's how," she says. "Let's go finish her."

I watch her walk back to the shed, the moonlight casting a glow over the yard and my eyes travel over her hips, swaying as she walks with purpose to the killing den.

"Hurry up," she says loudly as I follow slowly behind her.

I smile as I see her opening the crate and holding the knife to her aunt's throat. "Run and I'll kill you right here. You can die sitting in your own piss and shit." Her voice isn't trembling tonight, and she is gaining strength from these kills. Janet still tries to run, but I grab her and hoist her onto the table, securing her hands in the restraints.

"Pretty sure my beautiful girlfriend told you not to run," I tell her as I put her ankles in the restraints. "She has stuff to say, and you are going to listen. If you decide not to, I'm sure I can find something to gag you with."

Her eyes squeeze shut like she can pretend this isn't happening. Marla uses the step stool to get closer to her aunt. I hook up the bucket to the drain. "All ready for you my dove, I'll be in that room," pointing over my shoulder. Kissing her cheek, I turn and walk to the little room.

Twenty

Marla

I watch him walk away as I tie the heavy black apron on myself. I don't see the point, but he has a problem with cleanliness, so I'll do what he wants. My heart is racing with excitement and my stomach flip-flops for the love I have for this man who will do anything for me. I'm thrilled at the way he cares about me and the ability his presence has to help push the darkness to the edges of my mind.

"You are disgusting, lusting over a man who thinks it's okay to tie someone to a table. A man, if you can call him that, who kills people." Janet ruins the moment for me. The past flashes before my eyes: every time she ridiculed me, every time she sided with my mother, and the parties she attended where she watched me be abused.

"Should I have loved you? When you told me I wouldn't make it as an adult? That I wouldn't be able to live on my own without my mother?"

She turns her head to look at me. "You haven't made it as an adult. You are every bit of the lowlife I imagined you would become."

Her words hurt me. I shouldn't let them cut me like my mother's, but somehow, they always creep through and dig little slices, as if her words were insulation, and I grabbed a big handful. I remember the time she partied with my mother, my siblings and I were banished to the attic, and they got me to play with the pink fluff. The cuts on my hands were so tiny, but painful.

No longer thinking of the memories, I slide the knife into her neck like Sebastian showed me, using more strength than I thought I had. Her blood pours out quicker than my uncle's, cascacading over the blade as I continue to apply pressure, slicing through the muscles and tendons. With the angle of the table, it flows to the small sink above her head. Red mixes with her white hair and stains it.

It feels like minutes, I lose focus and stare at the blood pouring out of her. The room spins slightly, and I feel powerful, but I've lost track of time as I press the knife harder.

"Marla, you can't kill her twice. You've done well, but she's long gone."

I glance up at him, then look back to Janet and I notice the life is gone from her eyes. The corpse lays still and the blood slows down. It covers my hand from the pressure I've applied. I pull my hand away as I look in his direction. Taking a deep breath, the air is filled with metallic overtones and dampness. "Go clean up. I'll deal with the mess here and then I'll move her body, but we'll cover them together."

I don't wait to be told again. My legs tremble as I walk towards the workbench, washing the knife and my hands. I take off the apron and head out the door. Once the fresh air hits my face, reality crashes around me like an explosion. I want to kill everyone who has hurt me, but the realisation that I've killed three members of my family in a short amount of time swirls around me in a weird, threatening feeling. I wonder what I've become.

While I walk over to the back of the house to lean against it, my chest tightens. I can't breathe. The air has been sucked out of my lungs and my blood has turned to a gritty glue that hurts as it pumps through my veins. Inhaling deeply through my nose only causes my heart to race faster, making me feel more anxious.

My gaze wanders across the landscape, taking in the sights and textures. The backyard is surrounded by a dense thicket of trees. I suspect the overgrown leaves on the trees are a deliberate attempt to create a sense of natural privacy. The vibrant colours of the flowers lining the yard catch the eye. The full moon casts a ghostly light that adds an eerie feeling to the shadows.

As I take another breath, I'm aware of the smell of fresh air, a cool breeze that smells of the country, the dampness of the vegetation, and the jasmine shampoo I use. Slowly, my mind takes in these details, allowing myself to become grounded in the moment.

I light a smoke and watch as he emerges from the shed. His footsteps are silent, and Sebastian drops down beside me. The sweet smell of his sweat against the metallic scent of blood surrounds him.

"Are you doing, okay?" I nod, filling my lungs again with a deep breath, the air better than when I first came out. He reaches out and steals the smoke from my hand, taking a drag without moving his eyes from mine. "When you are done, just tell me. You never have to do this because you think I like it. This is for you."

I know this, I know all of this, yet the depression fights with the anxiety, and the demons inside my head battle over what I'm doing. But when I look into his eyes, I feel the demons slightly recede into the dark edges of my mind.

"I know. Each time I feel powerful, but I also seem to have a panic attack or something."

He hands the cigarette back to me. "It's a complex situation. You've dreamed of this for years. Wanting to hurt people who have hurt you is normal, but rarely do you get to do it. I'm here for you. Let's take care of this, then we can head to bed."

We walk back to the shed together and he puts Janet over his shoulder like she weighs nothing. His strength both impresses me and turns me on. His dark hair falls in his eyes, and he grabs the large metal bucket that is under the table with the other hand.

"Do we need to clean up here?" I ask.

He stops and looks over the room. "Nah, I've done everything I need to do. You can turn off the lights and lock up." I do as he says and walk out behind him. Her body falls like my uncle, but doesn't make a thud.

Exhilaration runs through me, warmth crawls through my body and I wonder what is seriously wrong with me that I'm so turned on. Or does taking back your power fill you with lust? Sebastian hands me a shovel and we work together to fill the hole. I watch more than I sling dirt. His muscles move under his tattooed skin, glistening with sweat, and I want him so badly. Yep, something is definitely wrong with me.

"If you quit eye fucking me, we can fill the hole quicker and get to actual fucking." His voice pulls me from my thoughts. A wicked smile creeps over his face and I bite the inside of my lip to stop from laughing. Once we are done, he pats the top with the shovel, grabbing the second shovel from me. He leans them behind the shed and gets the metal bucket, and I walk with him as he feeds the rest of the plants.

"Where did you learn about the blood?"

"It was sorta an accident. One of my first kills. I had a bucket near the table and didn't know what to do with the blood that was in it. I threw it out in the yard and then, over the next few weeks, the plants grew so much bigger and better. After that, I had to scour through several auctions but was able to get a table like they use for autopsies. Over the years, I've gained more things." He fills the bucket with water, swishing it out as he grabs the hose and I follow as he waters the yard. Every few minutes he pretends to spray me, and I giggle.

"Stop. I can't wait to go up to the bath. I feel dirty."

His eyes full of lust and mischief meet mine, and he points the hose at me, drenching me from head to toe in water. I try to tackle him, but I'm no match for his strength. He turns off the hose and prowls towards me. As he throws the hose to the side, his hand reaches my hair and grips the strands in his fist, bringing my lips to his. In slow motion, we tumble to the ground. He lets go of my hair and leans back on his heels.

"Do you feel refreshed or still dirty?" he asks.

I look up at the sky. The stars twinkle and, as I glance back at him, he crawls towards me on his fists and knees. The moonlight makes him look more menacing than he is. His look turns feral as he reaches my body, shredding the shirt from my body and undoing my jeans before ripping them off.

I lay in the yard, wet grass and mud beneath me. "Still dirty."

He reaches behind his head and pulls his own shirt off. Reaching into his pocket, he pulls out a pocket knife and flips it open. I watch him through a haze of lust. I hear fabric tearing as he cuts the centre section of my bra and removes the straps. His lips find mine as he rolls my hardened nipples between his fingers, igniting a fire within me. With a sudden halt, he breaks the kiss and rises, straddling my body. As he tilts his head and looks down at me, he runs the blade from my ear to my chin, tracing my skin with the knife without breaking eye contact.

"You are so fucking hot. I don't deserve you for one minute, but I'm going to enjoy every second of you." His voice is rough.

Sebastian's hand rests on my throat as he angles my head up so I can't watch as he runs the metal over my chest, running it over the flesh, and as he reaches the nipple, I gasp.

Heat pools to my lower half and my entire body is on edge, waiting for him to make a move of some sort. Between his lips, tongue and the knife's edge I'm trembling under him, on the verge of begging him to let me come. His laughter fills my ears and he pulls his hand away from my throat, moving it down and sliding my panties over.

"You smell fucking amazing. I could devour you and I'd never regret it. My little dove, so turned on...your wetness is all I can feel."

He uses the knife to cut off the red panties. It's all I can do to not arch towards him, seeking pressure of any kind. His fingers roughly hold open my thighs. The bite of pain from them rolls through me, then his mouth is against the sensitive skin of my inner thighs as he bites me, gently at first, then harder.

"Ah, fuck. Please let me come. I need you," I beg. Pleasure courses through me, and I'm just shy of being able to fall over the edge. His flattened tongue runs over my slit, tasting my wetness and pulling me further into a frenzy.

Sebastian lets me go and stands, putting the knife away. He peels off his pants and flips me over onto my stomach as he crawls over me. His hands raise my hips and he slides his length into me, inch by inch. I feel everything, pressing my legs together to make everything tighter. I arch my hips and he is deeper than I ever thought possible. Sebastians warm body is pressed against my back, drenching me with sweat. Sebastian fucks into me hard, with each thrust, I'm so close to the edge. His hand fisted in my hair, he raises my head. His breath is on my neck as his tongue runs over the edge of my ear.

"Just like that. So fucking good," he growls, and I come all over his cock. His other hand wraps around my throat and he squeezes as he continues to slide into me, his cock stretching me as he gets closer to climax.

The edge of my vision clouds with black dots. Fear mixes with pleasure and, as I look at the yard ahead of us, everything combined is too much and I cry out in orgasm. He growls as he fills me, it's fucking divine.

"I love you, Marla. You are my person, everything I could have ever asked for, the only human in the world to ever understand me, you accept all of me, your body perfectly made for mine." His words fill my eyes with tears, his hands leave me, and he picks up our clothes before lifting me over his shoulder and walking into the house.

I'm in a daze as he walks up the stairs. He fills the bathtub and puts me in it.

All I can say is, "I love you, Sebastian. I could never have imagined I'd find someone like you." The night has caught up with me and I can't focus as much as I would like.

"I know my dove." He washes my hair, rinsing out the bubbles and dirt, pulling sticks from the strands. The water gently rocks as he eases himself in behind me and his hands run a cloth over my body. Afterward, he just wraps his arms around me. Him taking care of me is exactly what I love.

Twenty-One

Sebastian

It's been a week since we killed her aunt and uncle and she seems to be better. I haven't brought her back to her apartment, I think she is finally comfortable here. We should probably talk about it, but if she wants to keep both places, I don't really give a shit.

I dropped her off at the centre this morning. I keep trying to get her there earlier, but it doesn't seem to make a lick of difference. Being early or on time doesn't get you noticed. We've talked about how it's utter bullshit. I think the numbers start high, as I've never seen or heard about anyone getting a low number. The system is set up to fail, no one is actually getting help. Before we fell asleep last night, I asked her if she still wanted that water fountain, but apparently, with the newfound knowledge of the bodies, she doesn't think it needs it.

There are a few things I need to do before I can go pick her up. As I pull into the driveway of the supplier's house, I'm surprised by the gates and the tree-lined laneway. I shouldn't be because he's a stark contrast to Clyde, but I didn't seem to realize how loaded he really was. Two guards stand in front of the matched metal front doors. Parking my car, I get out and walk up the steps.

"Hey, I have an appointment with Mr. Sharp. I'm Sebastian."

The one on the left only nods before opening the door and walking through it. I follow behind him before being seated at a long table.

"Mr. York, how are you today?"

A man with an air of authority, who I assume is Mr. Sharp, walks in from the side door. He is wearing dress pants and a loose button down, his dark brown hair and moustache professionally trimmed. "I'm well, thank you, yourself?"

"Quite good. Do you know why I pulled you in here today?" The hair on my neck stands up. I consider if this is a trap, a way to get me off the board. I didn't even tell Marla how much I loved her this morning.

"Not a clue, I don't believe I'm behind," I tell him.

His light laugh fills the room. I grit my jaw, calming my nerves. "Relax. If I was gonna kill you, I would have had you brought to the garage or the backyard. I don't want your brains across the expensive rugs."

I take a breath and lower my shoulders, doing my best to smile.

"You aren't behind. You are the best drug runner in the city–better than Clyde. I have a proposition for you." I lean back in the chair, resting my hands on the tabletop as he continues. "I know you've been running crack for a while, that downtown core is great for it. I'd like you to run coke to the upper crest. You'll be working more hours. Is that doable?"

I nod. "Yes, sir."

"Excellent. Steve will be messaging you shortly with drop locations and where to meet in the future. If you need anything from me, here is my card."

I take it from him and bid farewell before walking back out to my car. This could give me the money to give Marla the life she deserves. With enough hard work, I could offer the same level of mental care that only the wealthy can afford.

When I'm in the car, I check my phone, noticing the text from Marla. She wants to go ahead with her sister. I wish she would have listened to me about taking our time. The detectives are going to put things together, or at the very least amp up the investigation, but I drive to her sister's house anyways

When I pull onto the road, I watch her sister filling the back of a moving truck. It's a bad day to grab her. As I sit in the car, my eyes remain fixated on the scene unfolding before me. The truck sets off, and I tail it, watching it steadily approach her mother's house.

Although I shouldn't, I drive down the street and see two moving trucks along with the same guy from that day we were here. I continue down the street and take the exit to the highway headed back to town.

Marla will not like it, but I have a different idea. If they are both moving into the house that is a museum of her trauma, the ghosts in the walls and the dark cloud over it, we should kill two birds with one stone and burn the motherfucker to the ground with both of them inside.

As I turn onto the road, she's waiting for me in the park, her dark hair over her shoulder. She's looking down at her phone, scrolling through whatever, her shoulders slumped. I can tell it's been another shit day at the centre. When her head lifts, her hazel eyes meet mine. A smile crosses her lips, and she gets off the bench and walks to the car. As she's setting in, I lean over to kiss her.

"I have bad news and good news," I tell her as I drive towards the flower store. I promised we would go this afternoon when she was done at the clinic so she could pick out flowers for her aunt and uncle.

"Bad news first, I guess," she says, opening the centre console and pulling out her cigarettes. She lights one, hands it to me, and lights a second.

"I didn't grab your sister today. I pulled up after my work meeting and she was all packed into a moving truck."

She sighs, blowing out a plume of smoke. "Fuck."

I pull into the parking lot and park, turning to her. "Good news: I drove to your mother's house and both your brother and sister were moving in."

"How is that good news? They sure wasted little time. Jesus Christ, no one has even called me." Her face reddens, and I can see the hint of tears forming in her eyes.

"It's our time to shine. We'll burn that fucking house of suffering to the ground." I grin at her. I know we run the risk of being caught, but after this we should let the trail go cold for a while. Everyone will be gone, and we can move on with our lives.

"Okay, will we do it soon? How did your business meeting go?"

We finish smoking. "We will do it soon. It was alright. I'm going to have to work more nights, but I'll be home by midnight, and I'll be making more money."

I get out of the car and she puts her hand in mine. We walk through the aisles and look at the different flowers. "Those are my favourite, but I don't want them for this." She points to the pink dahlias, and I smile. They have always been a favourite of mine, but they were far too pretty to cover the dead. She moves over to the burgundy dahlias and picks up a few pots of them.

"Excellent. We'll get them home, plant them, and then have dinner."

"What's for dinner?" she asks as we make our way to the checkout.

"Can we pick up pizza?" I look at her. The steady diet of tacos, burritos and toast is getting old, but I'd eat whatever she wanted until the day I died if it meant she was happy. "Sure, that sounds good."

As we sit at the kitchen table eating pizza, she stares out the side window. The flowers have been planted, but she hasn't said a lot about what happened at the clinic. "Did anything happen today?"

She shakes her head. "Nothing, as per usual, just a slew of new people. I miss you being there. It made the time go by faster, but Jess and I have been talking a lot."

I nod. "I'm glad you have a friend. It is a dreadful place, the chemical smell is nauseating and always gave me a headache."

Marla sighs and takes a long drink from her glass of pop. "It's such a fucking sham. I'm so sick of waiting. They are eventually just going to deem me unfit to be a member of society and take me to the back room."

In a forceful motion, I leap from my seat and straddle the chair she is sitting on, tightly clutching the chair's wooden handles, located just above her head. "Don't talk like that ever again. You are an amazing person. If I can swing it, I'm going to pull you from the program and get you professional help quicker." I steal a glance from her before I press my lips to hers. She can't leave me. No one will take her from me, and I will do whatever it takes to keep her here.

"You can't do that unless you're making the big bucks. Even then they can still deem me unworthy."

I know the consequences, but I have to do my best—do anything and everything to keep her here. "I haven't had enough time with you, I need you, Marla. You are my heart outside my body, and I can't live without you." Her hand touches my cheek and I nuzzle against it. As heartless as I am, I can't do anything without her here.

"I'll do my best, I promise." She smiles, but it doesn't reach her eyes.

"Go up and have a bath. I'll clean up here and come up to you." I stand, letting her up and take care of the kitchen. Once I walk up the stairs, she's already in bed. I strip down to my boxers and get in next to her.

"I'm sorry, I don't feel like having sex," she whispers. It breaks my heart, all the shit everyone else has caused her, the tragedy they've left in the folds of her mind.

"Never be sorry. You know I want you for more than that. I love you, Marla, through the good and the bad, through the light and the darkness. Always, from this life to the next."

She rolls over and lays against my chest and I stroke her hair as she falls asleep. I wait a while for her to be in a deep sleep before I pull out from under her. Slipping out of bed, I grab my pants, put them on, and quietly leave the room.

Once I'm downstairs, I walk out to the shed. I've figured out the right way to design the metal. Earlier this week, I bought a gold bar. I've melted it and hammered it out. Waiting on the hot iron, I make scroll patterns when the gold becomes pliable and work on the ring itself. The other night while she slept, I measured her finger so it would fit perfectly.

The tooth is done with its finish, and I bond it to the centre of the design. After what feels like minutes of working on this, I realize it's been a couple of hours. Time always gets away from me. I set everything in the tool room. I wish this room was bigger, but it's what I work with for now.

When I leave the shed, I see her on the roof porch. She sits like a bird ready for flight, the swirls of smoke surrounding her.

"What were you doing?" she calls down. I climb the trellis on the side of the house, surprised it holds my weight, and pull myself up to sit beside her.

"Working on something special. What are you doing awake?"

"Couldn't sleep. Woke up from a nightmare and you weren't here, so I came out for a smoke."

I grab one from the pack, light it, and put my arm around Marla, squeezing her to my body. "I don't have to work tomorrow night. Do you want to do it then, or wait?"

"Tomorrow night sounds good. Do you think they'll be all moved in by then?"

I think about it and nod. "Should be. It's been a few days." As we stub out our butts, she kisses the side of my face and scampers in through the open window. I watch her get into bed and am reminded of the many nights I stood outside my dove's apartment and watched her live life without me.

"Come keep me warm," she whispers, and I don't hesitate a moment longer. Crawling through the window, I strip off my pants and get into bed next to Marla. The way her body curls around mine is something I adore. Jasmine fills my nose as she snuggles closer. If I could cut myself open to have her crawl inside my body, I would.

Twenty-Two

Marla

We've walked a long way to be in front of this fucking house again. Sebastian said it would be better on foot even though they don't have neighbours for at least five kilometres on either side. "How do you know how to make it look like an accident?" I whisper as we get closer to the back entrance. There was always an open back door in the garage leading to the basement.

"I don't, really. You know my speciality is draining bodies, not lighting things on fire," he rasps back. He might be the world's worst whisperer. "If we can get in the house, I will take it from there." We enter through the back door and it's unlocked. Karma is on my side.

The house is dark as we creep through the basement and up the stairs to the main floor. My muscles tense as soon as I walk through the door. My siblings have kept most of the god-awful collectables and knickknacks that were everywhere, boxes upon boxes line the living room. I walk down the hall and can barely make out my sister sleeping in my mother's bedroom. Nausea rolls in my stomach. It hasn't been long at all, and they've made it a home I'm not welcome in.

Just being inside the walls gives me anxiety. Flashbacks of a time when the house was filled with people, my mother shouting at me for everything I ever did and everything I would never be. Neither my brother nor my sister ever faced the wrath I did. They were always doted on, love expressed and unfortunately, they stood by Mother's side until her bitter end. We should have been a family, they should have given a shit through the years and at least given me a crumb of hope for any sort of love.

As I watch Sebastian wander through the house, I think of ways to make this seem like it was totally an accident and not planned. When I remember the many candles that my mother kept in the China cupboard for decoration, I pull them out and place them around the living room. I put one on the end table where the curtains hang down too low, another by the arrangement of stuffed dolls she always kept which are creepy as hell. When I light the candles, the edge of the curtain catches the flame and I watch it grow, moving throw pillows closer to the curtains.

I stand there, looking out the back window, the woods black against the light of the inside of the house. "Marla, let's go," Sebastian rasps again. At this rate he will wake everyone.

At this moment, I am grateful for their hoarding ways as I hastily gather more items to feed the growing fire. We walk carefully down the stairs. I can't think of how to make it look like an accident in the basement, but as Sebastian tugs at my hand, I have to assume he has a plan.

We make it out back to the woods. I trip over something and he catches me. Walking further into the trees, I look over my shoulder, waiting for the explosion I'm expecting. Sebastian stops me to lean against the trees before the opening to the trail that will lead to the car. "There isn't going to be an explosion, if that's what you're looking for."

"Why not?"

"Because it's already suspicious, but at least this shouldn't be ruled as arson. It is, but it shouldn't look like it when the fire department comes in to figure out what the fuck happened. It should look like your sister is an idiot. I turned on the stove's gas burner with a pot of water and moved things slightly in the kitchen, so it looks like they forgot about it." He scratches his cheek before reaching into his pocket and pulling out his cigarettes, lighting two before handing one to me.

"So, it might burn down?" I know my attitude sucks, but I'm angrier than I thought I'd be. "What the fuck? I need to destroy everyone who wronged me."

"That's why we haven't left." I glare at him the best I can in the dark.

"So they could escape?"

"Unless they suddenly get really warm, they won't know there is a fire." I know this is bullshit, because there were at least three smoke alarms in there. He nudges me and hands me the batteries.

"They won't hear a thing unless something else goes wrong."

I lower my shoulders and lean my head against his arm. "I'm sorry." I should have just trusted that Sebastian would have my back, he's proved that time and time again.

"No saying sorry. I know you wanted an explosion, and I'd usually give you anything you want, but it's been pretty quick with your family. And I'm worried they are going to hone in on you as a suspect." He really cares about me, I realize, as I switch my view back to the house.

I inhale a deep drag. Exhaling it, I hope they don't wake up. I watch the upstairs, searching for any sign of someone being awake. We seem to wait for a long time, but then everything happens at once: flames erupt from the windows and glass shatters. As I watch the orange and yellow colours lick the sides of the house, I feel calm. Black smoke swirls above the house, the shroud of darkness that has always surrounded the house bleeding into the night sky. It's ironic really, all the pain this place caused, and now it's being ripped apart by the flames.

"Ready to go?" His voice pulls me from the fantasy I've had for decades. Every sin, every word going up in smoke sends vibrations through my body. The feeling when you want something so fucking bad, and it finally happens...it's heavenly.

I continue to watch. Wood is splintering. The house groans as if the weight of the past is far too much to carry anymore and the fire continues to spread. "If they aren't dead, we'll come back for them, but I, for one, don't want the fire department to come and find you watching this happen."

After watching the brightness of the fire, I can barely see him through the darkness surrounding us. "You're right. Let's go."

I've been in the bath so long my fingers and toes have pruned. Tears line my face and fall into the water, and I can't explain it. I wanted this to happen. All my life, I have only wanted those who hurt me to suffer. I wanted them to lose their life.

"Drink some water. You've been in here for so long, I'm surprised the water is still warm." Sebastian's fingers linger in the water, and I refuse to tell him I've refilled the tub at least three times. He unscrews the lid and shoves the water bottle at me again. I take it and drink at least half.

"Why are you sad?" he sits on the toilet seat looking at me. Concern drips across his face and I don't even know what to say.

"I don't know. Everything is exactly as I wanted it. I guess I still have to grieve, even if this is exactly what I dreamed of."

"Makes sense. I was pretty fucked up after I killed my dad. I prayed he would die for years. Every time I got closer to eighteen, I thought about how I would do it. Afterwards, I was happy but sad too." It makes sense, but having to grieve for the people who mistreated you is such a fucked up thing. You shouldn't have to feel for people who wouldn't give a second thought about you.

He leaves the bathroom. Once I'm finished drinking the bottle of water, I decide it's time to get out. I drain the water and pull the towel around myself. After drying off, I slip on a long shirt I pull from his drawer.

"Did you want to watch a movie or something normal tonight?" I ask as I walk into the bedroom, but he isn't there. Walking down the stairs, my footsteps echo through the empty house. He isn't downstairs either, so I head back up to the bedroom and grab a blanket from the bed. I wrap it around myself as I settle outside on the balcony.

Sebastian walks out of the shed. Without looking up at me, he continues on until I can't see him anymore. My nerves run wild, the thoughts overtaking me that maybe he is tired of me being here. I haven't been home to my apartment in ages, and he's been going out to the shed often.

I've fallen in love with a serial killer and now I'm cramping his style. That can't be something he would take lightly. If I continue to be here, he's going to get sick of me, just like my mother said. He's going to resent me and stop loving me, just like they did. Fear bubbles under the surface of my skin and my heart beats faster as I realize they were probably right all along: I'm worth nothing.

"Get out of your head. It's a scary place in there," he says as he sits beside me.

I glance over at him, surprised at what he's wearing. "Are those suspenders?" My eyes drink him in, loose dark jeans, and black suspenders over a white shirt. The colour of his tattoos stand out. He wets his lips, drawing my gaze to his handsome face, the lip ring on his full bottom lip, the hair that falls in his eyes. Fuck, he's perfect.

"Yeah. Can't a guy just wear suspenders?" I giggle, looking down at the blanket covering me. Through the opening, I see his shirt that covers my thighs. "You look flawless as usual, don't worry about it." He looks out over the yard.

Taking a deep breath, he angles his head to look down at me. "I wanted to do this properly, the real deal, but it turns out we aren't proper."

"What do you mean? If I've been imposing in your space, you just have to tell me. You don't have to break up with me." My heart clenches in my chest, the air disappearing from my lungs, and I worry about his reply. His laugh is light, but this isn't funny.

"I'm never breaking up with you. There is nothing you could ever do in this life or the next that I wouldn't forgive you for. You are mine. I wouldn't be able to live without you. You are everything to me."

I sigh, "What is it then? You've been spending a lot of time in the shed when I'm asleep or busy, I'm worried that I'm just going to impose on you forever. You didn't ask for me to move right in, but I've basically done that. My mother is going to end up being right. You'll tire of me because I'm not worth the effort."

Twenty-Three

Sebastian

The mention of a breakup causes a spark of anger in my stomach, but her words about worthlessness are the gasoline that fuels my explosive reaction. If we hadn't already killed everyone, I would leave tonight to kill them myself, ruthlessly tearing each person to shreds that has ever hurt Marla. Everyone who has ever made her doubt herself and what she is worth. Because the truth is, she is fucking priceless, and I don't know what I have to do to make her see that. I don't know how to change her brain chemistry to show that everyone in the past is a fucking liar. I grasp her chin and turn Marla's face towards mine. My grip will probably leave bruises, but she needs to know how serious I am.

"Listen to me—my words and not the ones in your head. Every mother fucker who has ever had the pleasure of knowing you and losing you? They are the worthless ones. They missed the opportunity to experience the warmth and compassion of the heart beating in your chest. Every breath you take kills me because it's another one closer to the end of you. The only regret I have in life is not meeting you sooner, not saving you from the shit environment you were in. I love you. I've loved you since the day I first saw you and I will never stop fucking loving you."

Tears build in her eyes. I want to kick myself for hurting my dove, but she needed to hear what I had to say. I remove my hand from her face, feeling the warmth of her skin linger on my fingertips, and reach into my pocket.

"I've been out in the shed because I've been making you something. I want you to be mine for the rest of our lives. Marla, my dove, will you marry me?" Her eyes widen, . Tears rain down freely as she looks at my creation before glancing back up at me.

"Of course, Sebastian. I love you for exactly who you are. Since you've come into my life you've helped keep the darkness from clouding my vision."

After sliding the ring onto her finger. I tilt my head and capture her lips with mine. As I tug Marla up to stand, her body presses against mine, and I take a seat where she was, pulling her to my lap. With one hand, I embrace her, my touch lingering on the small of her back, as my other hand hastily removes the blanket, my fingers glide over her smooth thighs and slip under her shirt before I slowly lift it up and remove it from her.

"Tell me what you love about me?" I roughly ask her as I continue to run my fingers over her skin.

"I love the way you look at me like I'm the only person you could ever love." As I gaze into Marla's eyes. I know that it's true. She is the only person I could ever love. No one could ever come between us. "Your lips, I love them on me, or when you are listening to me, and you play with your lip ring." I lower my head to kiss her cheek, feathering my lips down to her jawline and into her ear. She shivers, goosebumps show over her skin and her nipples harden into pebbles.

"I love the way your tongue speaks the words that talk me off the brink, the same tongue that holds me on the edge when you want me to come." Her eyes darken. She bites her lip, and my cock hardens at the sight.

Tilting my head down, I lift Marla towards me and taste the salty sweat on her skin as my tongue trails down from her neck to her chest. My tongue caresses her hardened nipples, eliciting shivers of pleasure from her body. I savour the sound of her moans and the taste of her skin on my tongue as I bite down. She's putty in my hands, and I continue to draw my tongue over her skin.

"I love the way you react to me, Marla. Every time I touch you, you respond in such an intense way." I pull her closer to me and walk her in through the window, laying her on the bed. I drink in my dove's beauty, her flushed skin, and lust-filled eyes. Everything is for me.

I crawl onto the bed, caging her body with mine. I want to worship every single inch of her, to prove that she is everything I desire and could ever want. My lips brush the side of hers and she turns and kisses me back. Her hands grip my hair and it's too intense. I pull away from her.

Straddling her legs, she uses the suspenders as leverage to be closer to me. Her nails drag down my stomach and send electric shocks throughout my body. My grip around her neck tightens as I stare deep into her eyes, pinning her firmly to the bed. I lower my mouth to her jaw, trailing kisses along her skin until I reach her neck, tracing patterns over the sensitive spot with my tongue as she writhes under me.

"I love how your hands feel all over me, the way you can make me submit and crumble under them." I squeeze slightly with my hand around her neck. Leaning back on my heels, and lowering the suspenders, I take off my shirt and run my fingers along her chest, teasing her nipples while I look into her eyes.

"I know we're made for each other, the way you melt under me whenever I touch you. I've spent a lot of time dreaming of how you'd feel, how you'd taste. It's better than I ever could have imagined." I whisper as my mouth covers the flesh of her beautiful tits.

Lightly, my fingers trail over my initials cut into her skin, the only scar that should mark her body. Her hand runs through my hair until she can't reach me anymore as I trail down her body with my tongue. "I love the way you make me come. I've never felt this way before with anyone. You bring the nerves to the surface and drive me insane with pleasure." Her eyes follow mine as I continue lower, her bare pussy in front of me.

"I love the way you smell. The way you taste, and the way you quiver every time I run my fingers down your thighs." I trail my fingertips over her inner thighs, and she does her best to fight it, but trembles under me. When I spread her open, she's already glistening for me.

Not wanting to tease her tonight, I slide my tongue into her slit. She arches on the bed as I hold open her thighs, tasting her on my tongue and licking up everything she offers. As I curl my tongue and slide it into her, I use my thumb to rub her clit, bringing her closer to the edge. She screams out my name as she comes.

"I fucking love hearing my name come out of your mouth as my tongue brings you pleasure." I lap over her clit as her body quakes from the aftershocks of her orgasm.

Once I'm done playing with her, I climb up Marla's body to kiss her. The way she licks my lips to clean her wetness off my face only makes my dick throb harder.

When I roll onto my back beside her, she gets up and undoes the buttons on my pants. I help her peel them off, my dick springing to attention and hitting my stomach.

"I love the way your cock is always ready for me," she whispers as she takes me in her hand, stroking me gently. She spits on the head and continues to work on jerking me.

When she lifts her head and our eyes meet, I can see every ounce of lust and love in them. "I love the way every single fucking part of you makes my dick feel," I tell her.

Her hard nipples drag on my skin as she crawls up my body, her eyes never leaving mine until I feel her slit rub along the length of my cock. "That's it, grind on me. Make yourself come from my dick before I fuck you so hard you'll be sore for days."

Her eyes half close as she rubs her clit over the barbells. I reach out and pinch her hard nipples until she screams out again. Without letting her recover, I grip her by the neck and flip her over onto her back. Lifting her legs over my shoulders, I tilt her hips as I slide into her. Each inch is engulfed by her tight, hot cunt, until I'm fully inside of her.

"Fuck, I love you," she hisses out. I don't give her time to recoup as I slam into her.

I fuck her with long strokes until I can't take it anymore. As I lean down and fist her hair, slamming into her harder and faster until her tight pussy is squeezing my cock. My eyes roll into my head as I fill her with my come, biting her shoulder as I groan.

"I love you Marla," I whisper as we untangle from each other. Pulling her into my arms, I grab the blanket and cover our bodies with it as we recover from the intense orgasms.

"You made this?" she says after a few minutes, her arm stretched out so she can see the ring.

"Yeah. I bought the gold bar earlier this week and I've been melting it and hammering it out." I'm glad she loves it. I should have said I bought it, but I was so fucking proud of the work I've done.

"This is incredible. Where did you get the tooth, though?" Her eyes drift from her hand to my face.

Unease rolls through me, but if she really loves me like she says it shouldn't be an issue. "It's from a victim. I don't even understand it myself, but I've become fascinated by teeth. I pull them out and keep them."

She doesn't cringe away from me but doesn't say anything. When she pulls out of my arms, my heart sinks. She fishes the shirt she was wearing off the floor and heads towards the window.

"Let's go for a smoke." I grab my boxers and put them on and pull the blanket from the bed and drape it over her shoulders when I get outside.

"Did you ever sleep with any of your victims?" Her voice shakes. She hands me the lit cigarette as I sit down beside her.

"Absolutely not." If only she knew how long I'd been watching her.

"Good, then it's one of a kind, just like I asked for."

Twenty-Four

Marla

He looks at me like I have three heads. "Just wanted to make sure I was the only one who's gotten one of these, or that it wasn't some skank you fucked and killed." I exhale the smoke, watching his mind process what I've said. I've never been special to anyone in my entire life, and I wasn't about to repeat the past with the man I love.

"No. You are the only woman I've ever wanted. You light something deep inside of me on fire. I burn only for you."

His words and actions give me butterflies, something I never had before him. The edges of darkness have returned to my vision. Although he comforts me sometimes, I worry I'll never be enough for him. That I won't make it through this. I reach through the windowsill, and grab my phone and look at the local news. The night only gets better and better. I place the phone back on the sill.

"I love you Sebastian. Thank you for helping me punish them all. I don't think I could have done it without you."

"Was it fatal?" he asks. The cherry on his smoke glows as he inhales.

"Yeah it was. They don't have many details, but it says two victims."

He puts his arm around me and squeezes me against his body. "Good. At least you'll be able to sleep better tonight."

We make our way through the window and he wraps me up in his arms, his kisses the side of my head as he nuzzles into a pillow above me.

"Drink your coffee. I got a call from my boss and have to be over there today. When you're done with breakfast, I'll drop you off at the centre and I'll pick you up at the park," Sebastian says.

Walking through the house, he seems on edge, and I wonder if his boss is going to fire him. "Are you in trouble with your boss?"

He shakes his head. "Don't think so. Haven't fucked up yet. Take the ring off. You don't want to draw attention to your status. They don't need any extra reasons to mark you down."

My face falls. I wanted to show Jess today, but I know he is right. They will want to redo my initial information which can push a person to the very end of the line. I'd hate to go to the bottom of the list.

"What time do you work tonight? Is there any way I can go out with Jess after the centre? I promised her I'd go with her for coffee soon."

He paces the kitchen floor. I think he might leave a hole soon if he keeps going over the small space. "That's fine, text me. I can grab you when you're done."

"Are we okay?" I don't know why I would think we aren't. He expressed how he felt last night, but I know when someone is angry, they can be secretly mad at you and pretend it's something else.

"My dove, we are perfect. I'm sorry, I'm just stressed. I have a new boss and he's a little scary."

I laugh. My hand covers my mouth, but it's too late. He looks at me, pinching his eyebrows together. "It's just hard to imagine that you think someone is scary."

He chuckles with me, and everything feels fine again. We don't speak as I snag my purse. He grabs his keys and leads me out the door to the car. Once we're in, I light a cigarette and watch the smoke circle out the window.

"I might be a little creepy, but this is a different type of scary. Message me when you are close to being done with coffee and I'll pick you up. I have to work for the next few nights, but maybe we can have that date we keep talking about having. One that doesn't involve death or blood." His eyes are on the road but the smirk that crosses his face makes me smile.

"Deal."

As I step into the centre, the overpowering smell of cleaner immediately hits me, making my eyes water. Every chair is full, and there's no room to sit. As soon as I grab my number, I head to the back of the room and sink down against the wall, feeling the weight of another day ahead.

There is a large sign on the door leading to the back, bold black letters that say you shouldn't talk to the other people in the waiting room. If I could roll my eyes any harder, I would lose them within my head.

Jess sits beside me. Her hair is a mess again and I wish I could help her more. Before she says a word, I nod to the sign, and she huffs.

My phone buzzes in my pocket. I pull it out and read the message from Jess. I smirk and text her back. We don't send a ton of them because it's not really allowed, but it's better than sitting here all fucking day without a word.

By the end of the day, our numbers are nowhere near being the ones called, and the anger vibrates through my body. I shake as I throw out my paper number, I can't help but feel like everything is against me, as if I'll never get anywhere on this road of healing.

"It'll be alright, one day maybe we'll get through. It's utter bullshit that we aren't supposed to talk," Jess says as we get outside.

"I know, but we'll figure it out. I don't want to be a dick, but if I wasn't honest, maybe I would be a shit friend. Do you want to go to the hairdresser?" Her face pales while her eyes hit the ground. "I'm sorry Jess, I just know Sebastian was honest with me and helped me with my hair."

"I can't afford it," she mumbles, and I look over at her.

"I can." The glimmer of hope in her eyes makes something inside of my heart turn warmer than normal. As we reach a walk-in salon, I give her money for her hair, so she doesn't have to feel bad when I pay. She gives her information, and we sit and wait for her appointment.

"I know when I got my hair done, it was a battle I didn't know I needed to win." She smiles, but it doesn't reach her eyes. I'm hoping this will help her, just like it helped me.

My phone rings. I check the caller ID, but I don't recognize the name. Jess reaches out and squeezes my hand. I don't want to leave her, so I ignore the call to stay with her.

"Thank you for not leaving. I know that it's so stupid. Getting a haircut isn't scary. I'm safe here." My heart melts. I know exactly how she feels.

"Jess, it's no problem. I couldn't even make it to the inside of a hairdresser. Sebastian cuts my hair. So you are doing far better than I could ever do. I just want to be here for you the best that I can." She squeezes my hand again and then they call her name, she looks at me but gets up walks over, and sits in the chair.

After a half hour, she comes back to the waiting area and her face glows. "They thinned it out, so hopefully it doesn't get as matted and stuff."

I return her smile and we leave to go for coffee. My phone has rung three more times and I don't know if I want to answer it.

"Answer. I'll grab us a table." She squeezes my hand, giving me moral support, while I answer the phone.

"Hello?"

"Miss Lee?"

"This is her." I stand outside the coffee shop, fiddling with my purse strap.

"This is Detective Hoyer. I was wondering if you had a few minutes to talk?"

Sweat beads on my brow. "Yes," I answer, listening as he explains the fire, and how my sister and brother have passed away.

"Oh fuck, sorry, I just am surprised. I haven't heard from them since my mother's funeral. I didn't know they had moved into her house." My hand shakes as I hold the phone to my ear.

"I'm sorry for your loss, Miss, but we will have to have you come down for a few questions and see if you can help us fill the holes in our investigation."

The world spins slightly, the air becomes harder to find, and my stomach turns. I have gotten everything I wanted, but none of that will matter if I'm in prison. "Yeah, I can be there within an hour?"

We exchange goodbyes. I don't go in the coffee shop. Instead, I pull out a smoke and call Sebastian immediately after. "My dove, are you ready?"

"No, I'm fucking scared. Detectives want to talk to me. What should I do?" As I take a drag, my heart races, but my breathing slows to smoke.

"Breathe. What do they have?"

"I have no idea. He just told me my siblings died in a fire and they need to ask me questions to fill holes in their investigation."

Keys jingle in the background, and a car door slams, "I'll be in town shortly. Are you at the coffee shop?"

"Yeah, I took Jess for a haircut first, so we just got here."

"Order it to go. We'll figure it out, Marla. Breathe, baby." I don't know how he can be this calm. As I end the call and stub out my cigarette, I walk in to order and sit with Jess until he calls.

"I won't be able to stay as long as I'd hoped. I have to go talk to detectives. There was a fire last night, I guess. My siblings didn't make it." She reaches out, rubbing her soft hand on my arm, tears well in my eyes, and my throat is thick.

"It's alright Marla, I'll see you in a couple of days. I'm so sorry for your loss. If you need me, just call."

Our coffee arrives. I sip it slowly and look at her. "I'm worried they are going to think I did it. We weren't on the best terms."

We haven't talked a lot about our past trauma. I don't know why she is at the centre, and she doesn't know a lot about me. We've spent more time just getting to know each other as we are now, leaning on each other in the centre and forming a friendship. Although she asked about my scars one day when my sleeve pulled up, I haven't had to cut my skin in a while. I should take it as a sign of healing, but the wild desire I have for it scares me. The way I crave slicing my skin open again is becoming suffocating and I don't know what to do anymore.

"I get it. When my dad died, everyone blamed me for his heart attack, like I could have controlled that. That the life I put him through must have added to the stress. It's not the same as you, but I understand blame," she says before she drinks half of her coffee.

"Everyone blamed me when my mom ended her life, like it was my fault that she didn't like my boyfriend." The corner of her mouth turns up in a pity smile and I hate those.

"We can't save everyone. When someone decides to end their life, they have exhausted every option they could have. They have fought a battle we can't see and succumbed to the injuries of life. The time and thought that goes into those final breaths isn't something we will ever understand." Her words are hauntingly beautiful, even though I know I ended my mother's life. In reality, she would have never killed herself.

"I know we can't. I just hope this goes well and I don't end up in prison. I don't think I'll make it through that."

Her laugh makes me giggle, but I stop when she leans in close. "If you need an alibi, you can always use my name. I'll always be there for you." She pulls away just as quickly and smiles at me, looking around until my phone buzzes to tell me that Sebastian is outside.

"Do you need a drive home?" she shakes her head no. As we stand from our chairs, she gives me the biggest hug and we walk out together before we part ways.

"My dove, let's go to the detectives so we can get home. How was your day?" he asks as I get into the car.

"Okay, they put up a new sign that we're not supposed to talk anymore. Jess said I could use her for an alibi if I needed one, but where would that leave you?"

He is silent until we get about five minutes away. "Did they ask to speak with me?"

I think over the conversation with the detective. "No, just me."

"I don't know what would be better. If you think it would be better to use her, then I can call my boss and see if he can say I was working. I don't know what you want to do here?"

While we're parked at the station, I look down at my nails. "I just don't want to go to prison. I don't want them to look at us and think it was us because of what happened with my mother. God, and whenever they figure out that my aunt and uncle are missing."

"Then use Jess. I'll stay here when you go in and make a call." I run my hands through my hair and decide what I'll do. I get out of the car and close the door.

"Okay, I'll be back. I love you, and I regret nothing." I look back into the car before I walk away. His eyes darken, and he wets his lips.

"I know. I love you, Marla."

Twenty-Five

Sebastian

As I watch her walk away, I think about that night. We wore gloves, and they shouldn't have any sort of evidence tying us back there. Both of us have been there before in a friendly context. Everything looked like an accident except for the batteries, but that could have been normal for a house. I know my father used to pull the smoke alarm batteries out for months on end because he couldn't cook worth shit.

I don't want to bother Mr. Sharp again today. Our meeting was fine, but I don't want to fuck up a good thing. Instead I dial Steve, waiting for him to pick up. I tap my fingers on the steering wheel.

"What's up?" he asks when he answers.

"Hey, I need a favour. I can work for free for a bit, or I can owe you."

"Depends on what it is. Hurry up, I'm about to pick up for tonight's drop."

"I need an alibi for last night." Exhaling, I wait for an answer. Nerves churn my stomach.

"Alright, you were with me last night. You owe me in the future."

Before I can say thanks, he ends the call. I don't know what I'll owe him, but if it means we're both free, that's all that matters. I light a smoke, waiting for her to come back out. Checking the surroundings, restlessness works its way into my legs. The last place a person like me should be is in the police station parking lot. Pulling up my phone again, I look over the news for the last few days. When I look up to put out another smoke, I see her walking out.

Her jeans hug her hips perfectly. She's so fucking hot. The long black sweater she's wearing hides her completely. Marla fidgets with her hair and bites her red lips. I watch her eyes scan the surroundings. She looks guilty as hell.

I smirk to myself as she gets into the car. Tears line her face, she sniffles, and before we can sit here any longer, I drive out of the parking lot to get us home.

"How'd it go?" I ask once we are away from the station.

"It was alright. They asked if I knew what Ashley and Michael were like, if they were forgetful. I told them they often forgot several things, but I didn't know they were even living there. We talked about where I was last night, and they called Jess to confirm, which she did."

"Are your tears real?" If they hurt her, I don't know what I'll do because I don't want to lose her, but I'll fuck shit up.

"Nah, performance of a lifetime again. I thought about everything they ever did when we were growing up and it made it easier for them to flow."

"Proud of you. Now that it's in the past, we can move forward. We'll slow down on the killing and be law-abiding citizens for a while, just live life. I made pasta for dinner. I ate before I came to get you, because I have to go out for work tonight."

"I have a lot of work to catch up on, so I'll be busy," she says.

As we pull into the driveway, I look over at her. "I have time for dessert though." Cocking my eyebrow, she laughs softly.

She gets out of the car and scampers into the house. I follow closely behind her and grip the back of her neck when we enter the kitchen. "I missed you today. I know we're together too much, but it just felt lonely here without you," I rasp into her ear, pulling the sweater up and over her head. Her bare skin is warm under my hands.

Marla tries to turn to look at me, but I hold her in place. "Braless? What are you trying to do to me?" Her back arches, trying to connect with me.

"You keep fucking cutting all my clothes. I'm going to run out," she breathes.

I lean her against the counter, wishing I had my knife right at this moment because I would trail it all over her body. Hearing her fearful gasps is my favourite, knowing she is perfectly safe with me. The way she turns me on doing nothing is insane. Her voice, her scent, everything surrounds me, and I growl with desire. I kneel behind her, ripping down her jeans. I grip her hips as I press her to the counter.

"Stay perfectly still for me. If you move, I'll wait until I get home to make you come." Although I think I'll do that anyway. I part her legs with my hands and run my fingertips over her skin. As I inhale her scent when I press my face against her opening, I sink my fingers into her, coaxing the wetness I know is there.

While I explore her with my fingers, my other hand pinches her clit and I listen for her gasps. Spreading her legs to their maximum, I spin around so I'm directly under her as she almost rides my face. I tongue fuck her and rub against her clit until she shatters over me. When I pull away, I use the kitchen cloth to clean my face.

Needing to get going to meet Steve, I pull her jeans back up and spin her around to face me. My hands slide over her cheeks as I draw her in for a kiss, letting her taste herself on my tongue.

"What about you?" she asks as we part.

I smile. "I'll get mine when I'm home from work. Be good."

I watch her lazily put on her sweater before she grabs her stuff and walks away to go upstairs.

"Be safe. I love you," she calls out as she walks up the stairs.

I grab my keys out of my pocket and head to the meeting to pick up with Steve.

The night passes quickly. The customers for the blow are much better than the downtown core that lives and breathes for crack.

It's just after midnight when I get home. The kitchen has been cleaned up from dinner and the silence is deafening. I didn't think I'd ever get attached to being with her so much that being alone seemed unnatural.

As I get in the shower, I think about earlier. Everything about her turns me on. The way she lets go under me makes my dick throb, however I miss the thrill of getting caught. I used to feel it so often when I was stalking her. Ideas cross my mind. As I towel off and move to the bedroom to grab a pair of sweatpants, my eyes drift over her form, her hand on my pillow. The ring looks perfect on her finger. Her curves are covered by the thin sheet.

While I stand there watching her sleep, I stroke myself through my pants. Before I do anything else, I walk out of the bedroom to go to the shed where I grab my favourite knife. On my way back to the bedroom, something catches my eye in the living room.

Underneath a pile of books and papers, I find a blade that isn't mine. The back of my neck heats as the rage fills me. She has cut her perfect skin without me. The idea of her falling through my fingers pisses me off and I race up the stairs as quietly as I can.

When I enter the bedroom, she is still sleeping. Although irritation fills me, I creep next to the bed. Slowly I pull the sheet off of her, raising her sleeve and see nothing but scars.

As she stirs, I'm overcome with possession, and before she can open her eyes, I'm on the bed with the knife in one hand and my chest pressed against the back of her head, I angle the blade, sharp side away, as I lower it across her throat. Her eyes fly open in fear, her fingers fly up to the blade, but I hold both her hands down.

"Don't fight me, just tell me the truth. Did you hurt yourself tonight?" She relaxes against me, but the alarm stays in her eyes as she looks up at me. The side table light shimmers off the blade.

"No. I thought about it, but I didn't do it," she whispers. My darling dove's voice trembles even though she knows I would never hurt her.

"Prove it, show me." I pull back as she rolls onto her back to lift both sleeves. No fresh cuts line her arms.

"Why did you want to hurt yourself?"

"The craving is too much. I thought about it for hours but decided I'd never be able to hide it from you, so I went to bed instead." Her voice is filled with sorrow, and regret lines her face.

"I'm proud of you. I know you want to feel numb and block out everything, but it's only temporary." Her eyes don't leave mine as she sits up and peels off the shirt completely.

"Will you do it?" Her eyes are pleading. I want to give her whatever she wants, even if it means I hurt her a little. I lean over and kiss her forehead. The pain that fills her face hurts me deeply, I'd do anything to give her a release.

I get off the bed and strip down. Setting the blade down on the bedside table, I throw the sheets and blankets on the floor, I prowl towards her on my hands and knees and kiss her lips, feeling the urgency of her wants and needs as she grasps the back of my head and pulls my hair hard. Lowering my mouth to the column of her neck, I feather her with kisses until she moans. Moving down to her breasts, I lick between them and take each nipple in my mouth, sucking and biting her until her back arches and her body presses into mine.

"Fucking perfect," I whisper as I reach across to the side table and grab the knife handle. I run the tip of the blade over her skin. The way the skin puckers under the point drives me crazy.

My initials above her heart have faded into red and purple scarring. Using the blade tip, I apply slight pressure across her stomach. Her gasp fills my ears and I continue trailing her body until I reach above her perfect pussy.

"You aren't doing what you said you would," she says in an angry tone.

It's true, but I never said I would do what she wanted, either. I grip the handle as I bring it back to her chest. I press down as I pull the sharpness across her flesh. A perfect line appears under her breast, blood beading as the skin opens, and I watch it drip down her stomach.

The rise and fall of her chest quickens and I look up towards her face. Ecstasy fills her eyes and her teeth bite down on her bottom lip. I create another line under the first. I watched her for so long to know exactly the way she did it to herself. After the third, I'm done hurting her. As much as she wants this, I don't want to take it too far. Placing the knife back on the table, I lower my head and lick up everything that is running out of her, all of her life essence is mine, it belongs to only me.

As I make my way up her body, I slide my hardness through her folds and her wetness coats me. While I kiss her and lick her skin, my dick throbs. She tenses under me as I grind against her. I place my mouth over hers, covering her moans with my lips.

When I can't take it anymore, I fill her wet cunt with my hard cock, shoving into her until I can feel her milking me. It takes everything I have to not pound her into the bed. Her breath hitches in her throat as I slide into her slowly. Desire fills her eyes and I lower my head to continue to kiss her neck, her collarbone, and her tits. Our fronts are both covered in sweat, blood, and her wetness, and I wouldn't change a fucking thing.

Her beauty captivates me as her hands slide into my hair. It's as if we can't get any closer to each other without devouring each other whole. I fuck her harder. Bending her knee, I hold one of her legs against her chest and rut into her until she crumbles under me, her perfect pussy squeezing the life out of my cock. I fill her with my come and kiss her again before I pull out,

"I think we might need a bath," she whispers under me.

As I look down, I chuckle. "Yeah, I think so. I love you, Marla."

"I fucking love you, Sebastian. Thank you for taking the edge off. I don't know what I'd do without you."

I nuzzle her nose. "And you'll never have to find out."

Marla

Life slowly returns to normal after a few weeks, and it almost feels like it did before I met Sebastian. I've made a few clients so happy that I'm on their full-time list. The work brings me joy, but I can't help feeling anxious that I won't meet their expectations and will be let go. Thanks to the freedom of working remotely, I can indulge in the luxury of sleeping past noon or spending a lazy morning in bed with Sebastian.

He's been working later and more hours, but he says it's for the best. I never thought I'd find my other half, but Sebastian proved me wrong. He is determined to give me the full experience of life, taking me on multiple dates that expose me to new sights, sounds, and tastes.

As I grab my long sleeve shirt and struggle with it over my head in the dark room, my phone buzzes and doesn't stop. I grab it quickly off the nightstand and do my best to not fall down the stairs. "Hello?" I whisper, not wanting to wake Sebastian. He works tonight, and we were up late.

"Hey Marla, it's Lacy. Have you heard from my parents?"

Taking a moment to compose myself when I get to the bottom of the stairs, I reply, "No, I thought they had gone on vacation?"

My cousin never calls me. The fact they are now looking for Uncle Don and Aunt Janet makes me uneasy. They wouldn't be able to pin it to me. We didn't have a relationship for years. I don't see how that would come full circle to me.

"It's just weird. I haven't heard from them. They didn't come to the funeral for Michael and Ashley either."

"I'm sorry. I barely remember the funeral, it was all a blur, really." I didn't want to go to that either, but Sebastian said keeping up appearances was a good idea. That I wanted to create the image of a grieving sibling who had been stripped of everything.

She sighs through the phone. "I know. I'm sorry. Did they ever figure out what caused the fire?" I cradle the phone between my ear and neck as I pour the cold brew coffee into my cup and mix sugar into it.

"Apparently Ashley had left candles burning, and they said somebody left a pot on the stove to cook or something, but forgot about it." I sigh, remembering the call from the fire chief telling me they had ruled it accidental, and they were closing the case.

"If you hear from either of my parents, can you tell them to call me?" her voice trembles.

I know it must be hard to worry that your parents have just up and left you. "Will do. Take care, okay?"

"Yeah, you as well."

I end the call and move out to the backyard, curling into the chair that Sebastian bought for me. Unease creeps into my thoughts and won't let go. I can't even explain what is wrong. My mind is clouded with darkness, leaving me feeling drained and unmotivated. I sit in my chair, staring out into the backyard. The vibrant colours of the flowers bring me a sense of tranquillity as I sip my iced coffee. The phone rings again. It's never had so many calls in one day.

"Hey."

"Hey Marla, I'm sorry for calling," Jess's voice is flat.

"Never be sorry. I'm always here for you."

"I know, but you are supposed to have a date tonight, right?"

I think it over. Checking the time, I see it's past four, which explains the caffeine withdrawal headache. "Doesn't matter. Whenever you need me, I'm available. What's wrong?"

"I don't even know. Stupid, right? I just felt extremely lonely and thought I should reach out to you. It's nothing important. I shouldn't have bothered you. It isn't as if we can be fixed."

I knew that feeling all too well. "Do you want me to come over? We can just chill all afternoon and go to the centre together tomorrow?"

"No, I couldn't ask that of you. I know that you've been looking forward to your time with Sebastian. I'll be alright and we have tomorrow. Plus, every other day after that." Her laugh is forced.

"What if I come after dinner? We can watch television and occupy each other's minds?"

"Marla, it was a moment of weakness. I'm sorry I reached out. I'm okay, really."

But I know she isn't. After we hang up, I walk back into the house.

"Good afternoon, my dove. What's wrong?" I walk into his arms. They drape over me, holding me close to his warm body, so I'm breathing in his citrus smell.

"Something is wrong with Jess. She called but didn't want me to come over, but the feeling nags at me that she needs me. Also, my cousin called, looking for my aunt and uncle."

His arms go rigid around me, his hold getting tighter. "What did you say?"

"Vacation. I haven't had contact with them in a long time. I doubt I could be the first suspect. Fuck, their neighbours hate them just as much, so it could be them."

His head rests on mine. We're wrapped up in each other, even though I need so much more caffeine.

"What if I call Steve and go in for a later shift, we can grab tacos and eat at the lake and then I'll drop you off at Jess's. I'll pick you up from the park tomorrow when you're done at the centre."

"Has anyone told you how perfect you are?"

He smirks and pulls away from me to pour us both a coffee. "Call her and get the address and I'll call Steve." I kiss his chin before he leans down and captures my lips with his. Contentment and desire surrounds me as he grips me closer, but I break the kiss to walk away with my coffee and make a call.

"Marla, I told you I'll be alright," Jess says as she answers the phone.

"Well, I won't be. Sebastian has to go to work tonight. Apparently his boss didn't get the same memo you did and now I'm alone tonight." I'm hoping with the switch to my needs, she will want to help. I haven't ever gotten a call from her before, and I ache to make things better for her; she has quickly become my best friend.

"After dinner or for dinner? My apartment isn't nice, but it's…just…I don't know."

"What if we met at my apartment? If you would feel better about it, we can go there."

Memories run through my mind like a movie. I would have been embarrassed if anyone had come over when I was not at my best, but I got better at hiding everything.

"Would that be alright? I can meet you there around six. I'll bring chips." Her voice has become more animated, and I know that I've made the right choice.

"Sounds like a date. I'll see you then."

When I walk into the house, I see Sebastian dressed and sitting in the living room. He pats his lap and I curl up on it. "They are thrilled that I want to work on my days off. I told him not to get used to it." He laughs.

The disconnect I feel must be in my head, but I worry it isn't. His hand covers my wrist and his thumb strokes the skin under it, grounding me in the present.

"Get out of your head. You know it's a scary place," I lean against him, his warmth spreading to me. "What time are you meeting her?"

"Six, at my apartment."

He kisses the side of my head, "You are an amazing person, Marla. Not just anyone would drop everything to be with a suffering soul. You love so freely and fiercely, and it's everything I love about you." His words are tender but fill the holes that have been forming in my heart.

"I love you, Sebastian. Thank you for letting me do this tonight." His fingers are rough as they grip my chin, angling my head towards his. I don't let my eyes look into his until his hold tightens.

"I don't control you. You are not mine to keep. All I can do is everything in my ability to make you love me and hope that it is enough. You are enough, Marla. Everything about you is enough for me. Don't fucking forget it."

His tone is harsh, but his words mean a lot. I feel like I'm in a twilight zone where half the time I'm in the present living with the man of my dreams, and the other, I'm walking down the memory lane of hell with a mother who wanted me to be this dead inside.

"Now let's go get tacos and feed the ducks." I simply nod, unable to form words worth saying.

Belly filled with tacos, and more in the bag for Jess if she is hungry, I grab the grocery bag filled with caffeine and snacks that Sebastian bought. I give him a kiss. "I love you. Be safe tonight."

His fingers lace within my hair pulling me closer for another kiss, "I love you, Marla. Be good."

Jess is fiddling with her sweater and purse strap when I get to the door. "I wasn't sure if you had eaten dinner, so I brought you extra tacos. We also have snacks and energy drinks for the morning because I'm sure that my fridge is a graveyard."

She smiles. "Sounds great. Thank you for doing this." I shake my head as we go inside. I haven't been inside my apartment in at least a month.

We work together to pull my mattress out of my bedroom and lay it on the living room floor in front of the television. We spend the night barely talking and just watching different movies and shows, snacking, and at some point, I fall asleep.

It's still dark when I wake. I roll off of the bed and go to the bathroom. As I plug in my phone, I grab a bottle of water and check my text messages. After finishing my water, I set my alarm and get back onto the mattress, pulling the covers over both of us.

When the alarm blares, it seems like I've been asleep for four minutes, but I know it was a couple of hours. Jess is in the shower, and I change for the day. Stepping out to my porch, I light a smoke and drink half of an energy drink. Not having enough sleep for a centre day is never a good time. I've learned that time and time again.

"Thank you. The shower, the sleepover, everything was perfect." The way she words things troubles me.

"Jess, do you need a place to stay? Because you could use my apartment for however long you need." Tears fill her eyes and I'm afraid my suspicions were right.

"You wouldn't mind?" As the tears fall, my heart breaks. I love her and would do anything for her, the friend I wish I had met years ago.

"Of course not, we'll sort it out after the centre, alright? We can grab some groceries afterward and get you all settled." I have no idea what she's been through, but I can help control where she's going.

When I check my phone and see the time, I know we have to leave. "We better go. I can't afford the fine." I lock up and we walk to the centre together, grabbing some of the last numbers and making our way to the back through the herds of people.

"I think they've had an influx," I whisper, and she only nods. We sit, watching the newcomers well into the afternoon. I feel like I'm half asleep. Jess's number is called over the speaker. I look at her, shocked. Jealousy runs through me quickly before I smother the feeling.

We rise to stand together. I follow behind her as she inches her way to the front of the room. The door opens and three people dressed in light blue scrubs walk out for Jess, grabbing her number. The doctor pokes his head through the door and his eyes drag over us both.

This many people aren't needed for an intake. I've watched numbers be called before. I've seen people go in for their intake. I hold onto Jess's hand. I pull her back to stand beside me before they can touch her. "Ma'am, you aren't allowed to restrain other patients. You need to let number 52 go," one of them says to me. I look at the lady and memorize her face before I look at the others.

"Is this my intake?" Jess asks quietly.

"Miss, we'll talk more once we're past these doors." I don't like the way they are talking to her. Ominous vibes surround us, and I want to take her and flee the clinic, but I don't think she'd follow me.

"52, it's your time to come with us, we have to go," one of the women in blue scrubs steps forward and takes her arm.

"Do I have time to say goodbye?" she whispers to the doctor who has come through the doorway. I'm confused until it hits me, the way she has been acting, how she doesn't have a home and has been pulling away from me, they have deemed her as an unfit member of society.

"Fuck off. You can't take her. She has so much to offer, you can't possibly think that she is unfit for the world," I scream at their faces. More people in light blue scrubs come from a door I have never noticed before.

"It's okay Marla. It's just my time, I guess." Her hand grips mine harder and something inside of me cracks further, the pieces I've been holding onto for so long slice open my insides. The tears build in my throat and threaten to fall, my eyes burn from the chemical cleaner and my chest tightens with pain.

"No, it's not fucking okay, Jess. Listen to me, you fuckers. She is an amazing person. She is smart, important, and valued. She is my best fucking friend and serves the world by lighting it up with her smile. Have you seen her smile? Because it will make your worst day better. It makes everything better."

The doctor doesn't look me in the eye, none of them do. They pull on her arm and as I take a brief second I realize more minions in blue surround us, doing the government's dirty work instead of helping us out of the dark. They are extinguishing what little light remains within.

"Marla, listen to me. I love you more than words can express. Meeting you was one of the best things that ever happened to me. I am thankful for fate guiding me to you and bringing us together. Fight for us, Marla. I'll see you on the other side." Her tears stream down her face, and with that, so do mine.

As she accepts her fate, her grip on my hand weakens, and I can feel her surrender. She walks through the door and it closes behind her. As I bang on the door, my knuckles start to ache. The consequences don't fucking matter to me anymore. I'm willing to be thrown in jail or given a fine for disturbing the peace.

"This isn't fucking fair. Do all of you not see that? We all have something to give to society. How dare they take that decision from us? We all have a role in this universe and some man in a suit gets to decide if we get to heal? Or if we get to die?" I don't care that I'm yelling, the tears fall and threaten to drown me in my sorrow. Fury rolls in my stomach, and I realize I never told her how much I loved her, I never got to hug her goodbye and now I'd never see her again.

"Go sit down, or you'll be next," a gruff voice says into my ear. I turn and see the woman in blue scrubs. "Probably be the next on the list anyway," she mumbles. I wander to the back of the room where we were just sitting, like my life hasn't changed completely in five minutes.

I think about the woman's words, and how I could be the next one. I never want to come back, but the consequences are so high, I don't know what to do. The lady announces the end of the day and I watch everyone file out, waiting to see if I'll be able to see Jess or if they've already killed her.

"The centre is now closed. You can come back on your next appointed day," the lady says. As if I'm not the only one standing here and she's speaking to an audience.

I move out the door, I'm on autopilot as I walk to the park. Tears stream down my face as I sink down onto the bench to wait for Sebastian. Hugging my arms around myself, I try to take a breath. The gut-wrenching pain and fury build inside of me, and I don't know how much more I can take.

Twenty–Seven

Sebastian

When I pull up to the street where the park is, I see her sitting on the bench with her arms wrapped around herself. Her face is buried in her arms, but her body shakes. I barely put the car in park before I run across the park to the bench. The ground is a mess, but I sink to my knees to hold onto her legs.

"Marla, what happened? Are you okay? What did they do? Are you hurt?" I look her over but can't see any injury, though she's wearing a large sweater. She moves her head up and I can see the loss in her eyes, red-rimmed and hollow, and my heart sinks.

"They took her. They said she wasn't a functioning member of society and now Jess is gone." I blink away the tears that form in my eyes, unable to bear seeing her in so much pain, nothing I say can change anything and words are a piss poor band-aid she doesn't need.

"I'm sorry, my dove. Do you want to go home?"

She nods so lightly I almost miss it. I cradle her in my arms and bring her to the car, setting her down on her feet so I can open the door. Tears and whimpers continue out of her. I hand her a cigarette.

"I just can't believe it. We were happy this morning. We woke up and joked and I told her she could have the apartment because I stay with you and I just can't believe this shit."

I stroke her leg and start the drive home trying to make sense of everything she is saying. "Why did she need the apartment?"

"I think she was homeless, or living in a shitty place. I told her she could stay at my apartment for as long as she needed and there was hope in her eyes. She had so much to offer the world. How could they just rip her away like that?" I shake my head.

Like her, I hate the system, and I am just as clueless. "I don't know. What can I do to help you?"

She looks out the window, flicking the ash off her smoke. "Nothing."

"We can kill 'em all," I offer and her head tilts towards me. The wheels are spinning in her mind.

"No. Though, there is this one bitch, the one who ripped her from my arms. I'd like to kill her. I don't even know how we'd do that."

"I'll figure it out, whatever you want." After we pull into the driveway and park, she gets out of the car and walks to the backyard, sitting in the chair that I put there for her. I don't want to be away from her, so I bring a stool over and sit.

"The system is just so fucked. Why does it have to be this way?"

"I have no answers. The rich get richer and everyone else pays the piper for sins they haven't committed. Greed captures them all and those in need of services go without. Cutbacks everywhere have led to the epidemic of mental health needs being unmet. It's all horseshit, because people deserve help. They can rehabilitate everyone to serve society somehow, but instead, they plow through the delicate needs and fill our ears with excuses."

Marla doesn't say anything. Her eyes fall across the backyard and, although they are swollen, she's stopped crying. "Do you want anything to eat? I'll get you some water, otherwise you'll get a headache."

"Maybe it's what I deserve. I didn't save her and I should have. The least I can do is have a headache, some pain for punishment."

Pulling her out of the chair, I swiftly pick her up in my arms and bring her into the house. Grabbing a couple of bottles of water, I continue to our bedroom.

"You know, they made it painless. They have orders for that. She didn't feel anything, and I won't have you fucking punishing yourself for the faults of the government." Handing her a bottle of water, I set her on her feet before I pull her sweater up and over her head. Ripping her jeans off, I pull one of my large shirts over her so she doesn't smell like the centre. Laying her down on the bed, I pull the blankets over her legs and nestle beside her.

"I'm struggling to put a name to the emotions swirling inside of me. I've never really lost someone that I cared about like this. When my grandparents passed, it was because they were very old and it was a natural thing. Nothing about this was natural."

I pull her against my chest. Her makeup is smeared across her face. I kiss her forehead. "Listen, grief is a fucked up thing. It's going to come in waves. Sometimes you'll be okay, but sometimes you won't be. Your body just has to make room for the broken, bloated pieces of pain to fall into. It's like our bodies are made for a certain amount of pain and it just has to shake down and fall into the slots where it fits."

"How do I know how to act? I didn't even know her family. I'll never be able to say goodbye properly. I don't know what I'm supposed to do."

Her words bite at my heart. If I could swish away her grief like an Etchasketch, I would in a heartbeat.

"She knows. You know that. Everyone around you knows how you feel. You let us feel it. We know. And when you lose someone, anything you feel is valid. Want to get drunk and dance on the roof? We'll go do it. Want to kill some people because they took away your best friend? I'm your man. You want to sleep for a week and ignore the world? I'll do my best to keep you fed and hydrated. You want to shut it out and ignore the pain while we have crazy dirty sex for hours? It's all fucking valid and anyone who tells you differently is full of horseshit."

She only nods. I get up from the bed and get a face cloth, running it under warm water. I bring it to her to clean her face so that when she wakes up from the nap she desperately needs, she'll feel better.

A couple of weeks pass us by. I go to work and check in with Marla as much as I can. She's made it to the centre once, but otherwise I've been paying the fine. I don't care if she ever goes back. Marla chose the sleep-in-bed-for-a-week option, and keeping her fed and hydrated is a harder task than I thought it would be, but I've kept her alive. As I walk into the house after a rough night at work, I find her at the kitchen table, typing away on her laptop. Seeing her out of bed surprises me, but gives me hope.

"You look tired. How was work?"

We've never talked about what type of sales I do. I always thought it was silly that we have small secrets. "It was long, just a lot of horseshit customers. How is your work?"

"My clients understood why I was away. I felt bad, but I told them for the next while I'll have to go to work part-time. It's just too much and I know I should bring in money for you, but I've looked into subletting my apartment."

I shake my head. "Don't worry about money, just worry about healing. We'll be alright—not like lobster and gold flake cake okay, but we can still afford tacos." The smile that graces her face puts my world back on its axis and the tension leaves my shoulders.

Marla's smile fades and she meets my gaze. A fire burns within her eyes and she clears her throat and starts to speak. "I need a favour. I want to kill that bitch. How do we do it?"

I lean back in the chair across from her, thinking ideas over. "What if we follow her after work and take her from wherever she goes? That would work best if it's truly what you want to do. But it won't take away the grief. It won't fix what's broken, Marla."

"I know that. She wouldn't give me a chance to say goodbye and told me if I didn't stop, I could be next." Her eyes don't leave her laptop, but the rage boils under my skin and I grit my teeth. "Relax, you aren't an attack dog."

The joke catches me off guard and I laugh. "Have you met me? I'm your attack dog."

She giggles, and it's music to my ears. It has been too long since I've heard the sound. I watch her as she closes down her laptop and cleans up the notebooks at the table. "Want to go to bed?" she asks.

"Did you eat?"

She rolls her eyes at me. "Yeah. I had the leftovers you brought home at lunch." I purse my lips and raise an eyebrow. "I promise you I ate," she says, gesturing towards the empty plate on the table. "Today, I treated myself to more than just coffee and indulged in a refreshing shower." I wrap my arms around her waist and she sighs against my chest, grasping her hand I pull her up the stairs to bed.

"Goodnight my dove," I whisper into her hair as we lay down, her body pressed next to mine. Having her in my arms soothes my soul. Her face looks peaceful as she closes her eyes and falls asleep on my bare chest. Everything is right in the world when she is next to me.

"Which one is she? They all wear blue scrubs," I say to Marla as we watch from across the street.

"The one with the braid, the darker hair." We follow this lady home. Her apartment is in the same building as Marla's. It makes things easier for me, but we still wait for a while.

"What are we waiting for?"

"Just gotta wait a bit, can't just rush it, want to make sure she doesn't have a family that will report her missing right away."

After a few hours, no one has come. I get out of the car and cross the street to enter the building. Using my key, I slip into this woman's apartment and find her half asleep on a green corduroy couch.

Opening the bottle of chloroform, I wet the cloth and press it over her mouth until she stops struggling. I bring her down the service elevator and prop her against the pillar outside.

"Marla, bring the car around the back of the building. Hurry!" I say into the phone and then hang up.

The car quickly comes to the side door. As I hoist the woman into the trunk, I can feel Marla's eyes on me.

"How did you use the service entrance?" she asks as I pull away from the building, watching the city lights disappear through the rearview mirror. I look at her, "Because I'm the landlord."

"You bought the building I live in?" I nod, backing into the driveway as she just stares at me.

"I didn't want another creepy fuck staring at you. The only creep who can stare at you is me, so now I own it." When I turn my head to look at her, my smirk is wicked but her eyes are filled with gratitude.

"Do you want her to sit in the crate for a while, or do you want her strapped to the table? Your choice."

"Table. She can listen to me before she goes. Besides, you work tomorrow night."

It makes me laugh because we have all day to do whatever we want. "Deal. Get the doors for me." She opens the trunk and I haul the lady out, bringing her into the shed as Marla puts on the lights for us. Strapping her to the table, she rouses as I'm finishing the ankle restraints.

"You will all be fucked. Don't you know I work for the government?"

"We don't give a fuck if you work for the prime minister himself, shut the fuck up, bitch," I yell at her. Crossing the space to the small room, I unlock it to pull open the door, allowing Marla to pick her own tools.

"This is one of the many reasons I love you. You give me the creative freedom to hurt others any way I want."

While the woman is screaming, I lower my head and kiss Marla. It's been too long since I've felt the desire behind the kiss, and it's everything I need to reassure my doubts that I was losing her. She places her hand on my cheek and her fingernails dig in slightly as she pulls me closer to her. She kisses me harder and when she pulls away, I see lust mixed with the darkness in her hazel eyes.

"I love you, my dove."

Twenty-Eight

Marla

As I stare into his dark brown eyes, I know I don't deserve his love, that I'm just selfish and have been using him like a crutch. My love will never be enough to fill his heart. His lips spark the need I've been keeping buried over the last few weeks.

"I love you, Sebastian," I say before entering the small room and picking out a couple of knives from the wall. She deserves worse, but I don't want to waste a lot of time in the shed tonight. He hands me the heavy apron and, as I slip it over my head, he ties it around my waist. His hands caress me lightly and send shivers down my spine.

Dragging the stool over to the table so we can see each other, I lay the knives above her head and take a seat holding one. "If I don't show up for work tomorrow, they'll come looking for me!"

I click my tongue. "I don't think you are that important, there are so many of you."

"You psychopath, you deserve whatever is coming for you there."

"We live in the same building. Did you know you took my best friend that day? We had a sleepover the night before, calmed each other's fears, and watched movies. In the morning, we were hopeful. What did you feel when you went to work? Dread? Fear? Or are you sick like the government and feel nothing at all? Is it worth the money?" I have so many questions. We could be here for a week if I really cared about the answers.

"Bitch, you are going to kill me. Why would I tell you anything?"

"You are part of the problem, sure, but there are two ways to die. Quick, if I cut right here." I run the handle of the knife along her neck, and she flinches. "Or I let my fiancé pull out your teeth while you are awake. He's got a thing for teeth. I don't know why, but I think that might be worse than if you just bleed out."

Her eyes widen in fear. The smell of urine fills the air around us and I crinkle my lips.

"I didn't know. No one can tell if anyone has a life outside of that place. Yeah, the money is good, and when I first started, I really thought we were helping people."

"So, when you started killing people, did you think that was helping?" I cover the bottom half of my face with my hand until the smell passes.

"You become numb to it. The job is what it is." The rage churns in my stomach. One day she's helping and the next she's killing people for the sake of a paycheck.

"Was it painful for her?" I bite the inside of my lip until it hurts. I won't cry in front of this bitch.

"No, the procedure is pretty quick. We lay them on a bed and inject the medication. She wasn't alone. Two people stayed and held her hand, if you were worried that she was by herself."

That thought hadn't even crossed my mind and I feel like a bag of shit for only thinking about my own needs and not if she was alone when she died. "Does anyone really get an intake, or do you just bide your time until you can kill everyone?"

She sighs, like I'm taking up her precious time. "No, some people really get an intake and receive some help. It's not enough help for anyone's needs, but it's a start. We receive information from people who are higher up about the person outside of the centre and that determines if they live or die."

I'm disgusted and violation runs through me. Who is keeping tabs on us? If they watched Jess, then they definitely are watching me.

"I guess I'll make this quick. You'll be comfortable enough, but I won't be holding your hand." I smile as I lower the blade to her throat, pressing down as hard as I can. The metal disappears into her flesh. Blood runs over and I keep applying pressure. Muscle appears, but I don't stop until Sebastian grips my wrist.

"It's enough, my dove. You can't kill her more. I got this. If you want to go clean up, the hole is dug. We can take her right out after she finishes draining." I scan his face for disgust but only kindness looks back at me. His features are lax and his touch is soft on my skin.

"Do you think I'll ever figure out how to not kill this way?" I remember my aunt and how I took it too far.

"It takes time. It's a learned skill, not something you just know." He takes the knife from me and we wash up together. As we wait for her to drain, his hands work at taking the apron off of me. My throat clenches and I gasp for air before I run out the door to the night sky surrounding me.

As I sink to the green grass, damp under my knees, I inhale a deep breath of cool air.

"Slowly, remember. I don't need you to be in a panic." He never halts in his actions. Sebastian kneels with me, his fingers tracing patterns on my skin to comfort me. Anything I can give him is just not enough for what he truly deserves.

"In through the nose and out through your mouth. You got this. How do you feel? Did you get any answers?"

I think about the conversation I had with the woman. "Not really. She said they watch us outside of the centre. They have insider information about whether we are worth our life or not."

His arms crush me as he brings me to his chest. "Your life is worth living whether they say it or not. You are worth so fucking much, Marla."

Tears sting my eyes. I blink them away as I turn into his embrace, kissing his neck. I lose myself in his scent, the way his arm is wrapped around me, and the way he kisses back. He pushes me flat on my back in the grass and leans over me as his lips trail from my mouth to my neck. I've hungered for his touch for weeks. Time has passed, but his fingers pressed against my temple as he slides them into my hair reminds me of the first time we laid here in the grass and fucked like crazy. I memorize the way he feels, every kiss leaving an imprint on my soul.

"We have to go take care of her. When we're done, we'll continue this?" His question makes me realize how I've been lately, holding back from him.

"Of course. I need you."

He pulls me up by my hand and we walk to the shed. I hold open all the doors and put stuff away and tidy up. As we stand in the backyard darkness afterward, I ache for the moon to light our way tonight, but it's so dark I can barely see Sebastian.

"I'm out of shape. Digging holes is never a good time, but that really caught up with me tonight," he says.

"Replacing the dirt is hard, too." I know it's only half the job, but he doesn't disagree with me. I put away the shovels and we feed and water the flowers. After everything is done, I'm drenched in sweat and covered in dirt. Looking at him, he isn't much better.

"Did you want to have a shower first?" He doesn't answer me, but his powerful arms scoop me up and he cradles me to him before he lowers both of us to the ground. Surrounded by the death we've created, he props me on top of him as his hands grip my hips.

"We're just fine, don't you think?"

I lower my lips to his, tasting his salty sweat and licking down his jawline to his neck. The groans that vibrate as I continue to taste him thrill me. I push up his shirt and trail kisses down his stomach, and as I reach for his belt, his hands shoot out and stop me.

"My turn. I've been going crazy to fucking touch you," he says as he flips me over onto my back, tearing the shirt from me—another item gone to his brutish ways. He prowls over me like a beast going after its prey. His lips brush mine, gently at first, until he presses harder. Biting my bottom lip, he continues moving down my jaw to my ear before his tongue swirls on my neck. Sebastian's teeth nip at my neck as he trails down to my chest. Fingers run over my hardened nipples, and he lowers his head to suck on one as he pinches the other. His teeth run over the sensitive bud in his mouth, sending shockwaves through my body. Heat consumes me as he keeps worshipping me.

"You taste fucking heavenly," he rasps out before his hands hold my tits firmly in his grasp. His mouth moves down my torso until he reaches my belt, which he promptly undoes and rips out of the loops to peel my jeans off my body. He kneels at my feet, looking down at me. The edge of the moon outlines his profile from this angle, but I can't see his features and I want his eyes on me.

"Stop. I want to see you. It's too dark out here."

He looks around and takes a deep breath before he gathers me in his arms and takes me into the house. Once we're in the living room, he places me on the couch, pushing my legs up and open.

He kneels in front of me. As I look down at his dark brown eyes that simmer with desire, he moves forward and his tongue dips into me. I'm already wet and on the edge of orgasm.

"So fucking perfect. You are my favourite flavour in the entire world," he growls as he continues licking me. The sensations run through my nerves and I curl my toes as his mouth gets closer to my clit. The way he teases me drives me crazy with need. His eyes focus on mine as he licks circles around my clit. His fingers slide into me and fuck me as he watches me, tempting me to fall over the edge, but it's up to him. As he latches on it, I scream out, shattering over his tongue and fingers.

Sebastian is quick to move up my body. I taste myself on him as his lips catch mine. His tongue rolls over mine and I push him until he lies on his back on the floor. I straddle his body, needing his cock inside of me. Hands grip my hips as I position myself over him, sliding the head up and down my slit, coating him in my wetness.

"Don't tease me dove, you won't like the consequences," he says gruffly. His fingers dig into my skin as he tries to move me. As I sink down on his hard cock, Sebastian's look turns feral. He is stretching me, and I continue until he is all the way inside of me. I grind against him, gyrating my hips, each barbell rubbing inside of me against my

G-spot. As I throw my head back, I want to come so fucking badly, but I can't reach climax myself.

"You want to come over my hard cock?" I nod and lean forward, bracing myself on his chest.

"Come for me, Dove," his rough voice travels through me. I ride him, his cock sliding in and out. "Open your eyes. Look at me when you soak my dick."

When I open my eyes and look into his, the fierce connection rips through me as he reaches between us and rubs my clit with his fingers. I lose it, moans escape me as I ride out the shocks of my orgasm. I lean forward on his chest, his arms circle me, and I find myself on my back as his eyes stare into mine. His hand circles my throat and he thrusts into me. "You are so fucking beautiful when you let go. I love you so fucking much," he breathes as his hand tightens around my neck.

His lips move over mine, biting my lip as he fucks into me and I'm on the edge of pleasure when he pulls out. With a swift movement, he flips me over onto my hands and knees, and I can feel his breath on the back of my neck. His hands tightly grip my hips as I turn my head to catch him staring at me like I'm the only thing he's ever wanted. I move my hand down to my clit to play with myself as he thrusts into me and come all over his dick. As he passionately thrusts into me, I gracefully lower myself onto my arms, until he fills me with his come and lets out a primal growl.

Leaning over my back, he slowly pulls out. Sweat drips off his forehead as he looks at me. "Holy fuck."

I bite my lip, feeling how swollen they are, and smile. "Yeah, I love you Sebastian."

"I love you, my dove. Go start the shower and I'll grab our clothes from outside."

While he does that, I climb the stairs and then proceed to turn on the water. It isn't long before he joins me in the bathroom. We stand under the hot water for a long moment before he turns me to wash my hair, and I groan under his fingers massaging my scalp.

"Keep that up and we'll be going a second round." Once we're both washed, he turns off the water and hands me a towel. We dry off and get into bed.

"Do you feel better?" he whispers into my ear, as I'm draped over his body with his arms around me.

I know that for right now, at this moment, everything is perfect. "Yeah, it was just what I needed."

Days bleed together as they pass. Sebastian goes to work and I've spent a lot of time on the roof porch sending emails to my clients and thinking about Jess. I've collected enough fines that they will look for me at my apartment soon. As I lay in bed next to his warm body, I realize nothing was ever going to work out for me. It wouldn't matter what I did or how hard I tried, no plans were ever going to help me. It wouldn't matter if I worked harder, or healed more. I've been broken since I was a child, and it would take a miracle to put me back together. I've been selfish in keeping him tied to me. Our love fills me, but the darkness shrouds me, and as each day passes, the demons in my mind have been taking over all my thoughts.

"It's almost creepy how much you watch me sleep, you know that?" he doesn't open his eyes, but his voice breaks me from my thoughts.

"I'll start the coffee," I whisper. As I get out of bed and pad down the stairs to the kitchen I fix up the coffee machine and then sit at the kitchen table and light a smoke. Everything feels like too much and nothing at all at the same time.

"Want to get lunch before I go to work, which is apparently soon?" Sebastian walks into the kitchen wearing a dark green shirt with dark jeans. His hair falls over his forehead, but he brushes it back while he stares at me.

"Sure. By the lake?"

A grin forms on his face before he turns to pour us coffee. "Of course, where else?" He places the coffee in front of me and sits across from me, his tattooed hands holding the mug. He scrolls through his phone, and I take in every second I can. The way he fiddles with his lip ring with his tongue, the stubble lining his cheeks, and his dark eyelashes as he looks toward me.

"What's going on, Marla?" His voice is my favourite sound in the world.

"Nothing, just looking at you." I plaster the smile on my face, so he doesn't have to worry about me.

"If you say so, my dove. Go get dressed. We'll grab tacos and go to the lake." I stub out my cigarette and take the last swig of coffee.

Once I'm in the bedroom, I grab one of his band tees and pull it on, along with my last pair of clean jeans. Then I put on the earrings he made me and apply red lip stain. Finished, I walk down the stairs.

"If we woke up earlier, we could have breakfast." He cocks an eyebrow at me, grabbing his sunglasses and keys as we head out the door.

"Who wouldn't want tacos for breakfast, though? I mean, I think we're the ones doing the right thing."

His laugh fills the car as we drive to the same taco place we go to every time. I find it ironic we never tried another restaurant after the first.

I wait in the car while he runs in to get our order and watch him intently as he walks back to the car.

I watch his hands as they clench the wheel, and his face as he swings his head to look at me, and drops a kiss on my lips.

When we get down to the lake and sit on the picnic tables, we eat in silence, watching the ducks in the water, swimming in circles. I'm jealous that they know what their purpose is in life, they are born knowing what their life will entail.

"Marla, I'm supposed to have a meeting with the boss tonight after my shift, then I'm off for a few days and I think it would be good to get out of town for a bit."

"Yeah, sounds great. They are going to be looking for me, though." I finish the taco and put our garbage into the bag. He links his fingers with mine as we walk back to the car.

"You could just go. I'll pay all the fines."

"Do I look like I want them to kill me? Fuck that, I'm not playing by their rules anymore." His face softens, but he doesn't say anything, and we walk to the car.

"I didn't mean to sound insensitive, I just want the best for you." I look out the window.

"I know you do. I'm just too scared to go back." He drives us home. "I don't want you to live a life of fear."

After we get inside, I go up to lay in bed. Numbness covers me, and I can't handle the feelings inside of my body. He lies beside me, stroking my hair and running his hand over my arm.

"Are you going to be okay? I gotta go to work, but we'll do more fun things over the next few days."

I roll over onto my back, looking up into his eyes, moving my hand to his neck. His touch is gentle but firm, holding me close as we share a passionate kiss.

"I'm good, just tired. I love you. Be safe." His thumb strokes my cheek, and he leans down for another kiss. "I love you, my dove. Be good."

Once I hear his car leave the driveway, I grab my notebook and sit on the roof porch. I light a cigarette and think of the message I want to leave. My soul is exhausted, I don't want to make it another day and I don't want to crush him by telling him to his face that I don't deserve him. But the words aren't on the tip of my tongue. I've already messaged my clients to tell them I would be taking a long break. Inhaling a drag, I exhale and stare at the yard.

Tears fall down my cheeks. I wanted this to work so badly, but the darkness has consumed me, and I don't think I can wade out of this sludge this time. Once I'm done writing, I fold the note and put it on the bathroom vanity. Pulling the bottles out of the drawers, I take as many as I can, different cold medicines, sleeping aides, and everything I can think of to make this seem less painful.

I thought stepping into the tub with the blade would somehow liberate me from my mother's legacy, but it only amplified the irony of the situation. However, she is the one who laid the groundwork for this to be my future. If I had a mother that loved me throughout my life, maybe things would have been different. If I could have been stronger, then I could have survived the darkness, the demons in my mind wouldn't have controlled me. But I've reached rock bottom and I know my next destination.

I cut from elbow to wrist and watch the blood trickle faster than any of the cuts I've ever made before, while I still have the strength, I press as hard as I can on the other arm and relish in the pain as I lean back and watch the essence that is me trickle into the hollow bottom of the tub.

Twenty–Nine

Sebastian

When I get back to the car after finishing up with all of the clients, my phone vibrates in the front seat. It must have fallen out of my back pocket when I got out of the car. "Steve, what's up?"

"Mr. Sharp wants to see you. Meet us at 45th Street."

I wonder what is going on, but as I pull onto the road, I see a nightclub. The moment my feet hit the pavement outside, Steve pulls me into the side door. Darkness surrounds us. There is a private room that we walk to, and the music only beats through the floor and walls instead of being loud as hell.

"Mr. Sharp, good to see you," I say as I sit across from him. Nerves rumble through my mind, but I keep steady eye contact with him.

"We have a new runner for the downtown core. We want you to stay with the upper crest. You are a great dealer and I hear nothing but good." I smile as he continues talking.

"You will have fewer hours, but you'll be getting a pay raise, so it won't matter. What I want is for you to take this bonus, and take your beautiful fiancé on a vacation. She deserves it for putting up with you. And son, you deserve it for the hard work you've done."

Pride fills me. I've never been good at anything. His compliments don't fly past me and I take them to heart. "Thank you so much."

He simply nods and looks at Steve. "Go on home now. Have a good time. We'll be in touch."

I walk to the car, feeling lighter on my feet, and drive home. I'm excited to surprise Marla with a long trip that she deserves, taking her away from the toxic darkness that surrounds the town, the memories that haunt her, and give her the time away to heal. The lights are on, so I hope she's still awake. As I make my way through the house, I don't see her anywhere until I pass the bathroom. Seeing her head propped up, I assume she's having a bath.

"My dove, great news from the boss. I'm getting a raise and fewer hours. But he wants us to go on vacation. We can leave whenever you want," I call out as I empty my pockets onto the dresser.

There is no response and the air is heavy with the smell of metal. I turn to the bathroom, and as I reach her, I see what I've always feared.

"NO! FUCK! Marla, my Dove," I shout as I drop to my knees beside the tub. The amount of blood covering her lower body gives me answers I don't want. Tears cloud my vision as I do whatever I can to wake her up. Shaking her doesn't wake her up and I know she's not even here anymore. My fingers lower to her neck, the skin soft, but her pulse is gone.

I stand up and put my fist through the wall.

If I had just realized earlier today that she wasn't okay, I could've been here when she needed me. I could have saved her. I shove the empty pill bottles off the counter, realizing she would have passed out if she had taken these. The small comfort it brings me knowing she wouldn't have been in agony when she passed is like a band-aid that's too small for a cut.

There is a folded-up note on the counter. I open it and sink to the ground. Looking at her peaceful face, her eyes are closed and the sorrow is gone from her mind. But my heart has shattered. There isn't enough room left in my body for the amount of pain I feel. I look at the note and read.

Sebastian

My whole life, I just wanted someone to notice me. For someone to not push me into the background. Then you walked into my life and never left, and I couldn't have asked for anyone better. I only wish we could have met sooner, maybe then I wouldn't have been so broken. My pain leaks onto everyone I touch, and my mother's words will always ring in my ears, telling me I'm not good enough. I don't deserve love because I'm simply not good enough for anything.

Thank you for coming into my life when I needed you, because I would have been gone much sooner if it hadn't of been for you. Thank you for helping me rid my life of the toxic waste that poisoned me from an early age.

You showed me what love looks like, the one thing I thought I would never have. You blessed me with so many memories, things to remember as I pass to the next life.

I love you so fucking much and I'm so sorry that I have to leave you, but you deserve better than what I can give. I could never love as much as I think you deserve, and I hope you find someone that could light up your life like you did for me. The darkness has consumed me. I've been fighting for so long, and it was something that was just going to happen eventually. I'm so sorry for entering your life and for any pain that my absence will cause, but I can't fight anymore. I'm so fucking tired. You are such an amazing man. You are handsome and you gave me everything I could have asked for. I wish it didn't have to end this way. I love you so fucking much and I'm sorry.
Until we meet again,
Your Wren... I know stupid.

Marla xo.

Tears stream down my face. I push the note back up onto the counter, wiping my eyes with the back of my hand. I can't do this without her. I wish I could go back in time and love her harder and prove to her that she was enough for me.

As I stand up, I know she's gone, but I'm not ready to say goodbye. I pick her up, cradling her in my arms as I bring her to the bed, and I lay down next to her and hold on to her until I can breathe again.

"All I've ever wanted was for you to be mine, to fix your broken pieces, and for us to live a life together forever. I wish I could have loved you longer." After a while, she's cold. It hurts my heart if I have any piece of one left, but I wrap the blanket around her and fall asleep holding her close to me.

Days pass and she still lies beside me. I know this isn't what she would want. She would probably yell at me by now.

I pull myself out of bed. Making coffee isn't the same anymore since she's not here to drink it with me. Or maybe it's because it's not being drunk to keep me awake so I can watch her and make sure she's okay. I grab a smoke and light it on my way outside.

I find the perfect spot and start digging because, if she's going to be here, I'm going to keep her forever.

After I've dug enough down, I climb out of the hole and walk into the house. Wrapping her body with her favourite blanket, I carry her to the back-yard. While I slip her over my shoulder, holding her as tight as I can, I lower both of us into the hole and ease her into the dirt. I lay beside her, stroking her hair with my fingers, trying to memorize her face, and I choke on my tears. I press my lips to her forehead and climb out, lighting another cigarette.

I look to the sky for answers, but no one is going to answer me. Nothing is going to change, and I can't do anything to bring her back to me. It takes every ounce of strength to fill the hole. Grief grips me in an angry fist and my thoughts turn to black sludge as the dirt covers her and she's gone. I want to join her. The only way for us to be together forever is for me to follow her again, find her, and never let go.

As I lay on the grass next to the soil, I close my eyes and imagine a world where we live together forever and we never have to let go. Anger runs through my veins. The people responsible for this must meet their maker first. I can't just wallow until death finds me. My life would be for nothing.

I jump up and head into the house, changing into jeans and her favourite band tee. Grabbing my wallet and keys, I put on my hat and get to the car. Pink dahlias are what I need first. Finding them at the flower store, I drive home and plant them over her. I would have bought her every fucking one on the planet if she would have just stayed here with me. I pull my phone out of my pocket and call Mr. Sharp. Fear has left my body, and nothing is as dangerous as a person with nothing to lose.

"Sebastian, did you pick a vacation spot?" His voice is calm and confident.

Mine is thick with torturous grief. "I need a favour."

"Come to my house. We'll talk it over." He ends the call before I can ask anything more.

Checking the time, I see that whatever half-assed plan I have will have to wait until tomorrow, but it doesn't stop me from driving to his house. The guards open the door and I'm vaguely aware of what a mess I look like.

"Sebastian, what is it?"

My face must give away anything I'm feeling. "I need a gun." I exhale a deep breath, my cheeks blow out.

"Let's sit. We can talk this over," he says as he crosses to the table. The last fucking thing I want to do is talk about this, but I know he can get me what I want.

"We've talked before about how Marla goes to that mental health service centre, the despicable place that is. The night you sent me home early, I found her in the tub. I need the gun for reasons because I can't just–"

He puts his palm up. "I don't want to know who, or what, because it's an implication that I can't have on my shoulders. But I'll show you how to use it. Let's go to the backyard."

Relief floods my body. Without thinking about it, I follow him as we go to the yard. There are targets along the back tree line.

"We practice from time to time. I need to make sure all my guards have proper aim. This is a 9mm, semi-automatic. It doesn't continue to fire after you've pulled the trigger. Each pull will discharge one bullet. It offers more control and holds ten rounds plus one in the chamber. Each magazine will hold ten, but I'm hoping you don't need twenty-one shots."

I nod as he continues to explain. He shows me how to hold it. I watch him fire off some shots and he hands it to me. We spend the next few hours, until night falls, practicing and working on my aim. I feel confident that I have everything I need.

"Will you join me for dinner?"

I look at him, bewildered. "Yeah, I guess."

We walk into the house, his table already set, and a wide-set woman brings out two plates of chicken and potatoes. He smiles at her, and she disappears through a door.

"Thank you for this," I nod to my plate as I eat. I have not eaten much in days and it tastes incredible. Guilt follows that Marla isn't here to enjoy it with me.

"I want you to have a good meal, a good sleep, and see how you feel in the morning. If your mind hasn't changed, at least I've tried and I've spent your last night with you."

"I won't be coming back. I love the job and I'm forever in debt for you taking a chance on me, but my time is done here," I say as I take a drink of water from one of the many glasses in front of me.

"I know. Your eyes tell me everything I need to know. A man on the edge of death has nothing left to lose. The world is a cruel place, and it will eat your soul if you give it a chance. I'm sorry for your loss, Sebastian." We finish our meal in silence.

As I stand, he crosses the room and pats my back, handing me the gun and extra ammo.

"Good luck, son. You have made quite the impression on me, you have shown me you can't judge a book by its cover, because if I had, I'd have missed the opportunity of being proud for the first time in decades for the best worker I've ever had. You are someone important to me. I'm glad I had the pleasure to know you." He shakes my hand.

"Thank you, sir."

Every cracked piece in my heart splinters just a bit more, knowing he was a father figure I didn't know I desperately needed. But it's essential that I get back to Marla, because life is meaningless without our love.

"Thank you, Mr. Sharp. Your actions have given me more than I deserved in my lifetime," I say before I exit through the door. Walking to my car, I drive home.

Sitting in her chair looking over the backyard, I plan what I will do tomorrow.

From my car, I can see the sign for the mental health centre, its letters casting a shadow on the building's facade. Despite sleeping as best as I could, I woke up this morning feeling just as troubled as the night before. Marla is the centre of my world. Without her, my life is meaningless.

Since these mother fuckers added the kerosene to the fire that incinerated my life, they will all have to pay for not helping her the way she deserved. I walk into the centre, the chemical cleaner smell hitting me in the face. Many people sit in the chairs, lining the walls and I didn't think about the innocent lives, the people waiting for help they will never get.

As the door opens and people in blue scrubs come out searching for their next victim, I pull the gun from my pocket and tick off three of them. The rest scurry behind the door and everyone in the waiting room stands. "Everyone get out! Go live your life! Whatever is left of it is better than waiting around here!" I scream as they rush around like chickens without their heads. Finally, they are all out the door. I look around, but I'm alone.

I sigh. Eight bullets left and all the time in the world.

"Sir, let's talk this out. You don't want to do this. We can help you."

The laugh that leaves my chest is sinister. The doctor steps out of the door with his hands held in front of him, like he is going to negotiate a deal with me.

"Son, listen, we can get you help. There are more than enough resources to do so."

I don't hesitate as I aim for his head and he falls to the floor. I walk towards the door he came out of and find four more people in blue scrubs. Another doctor comes out in a lab coat and the fucking bitch who announces when everyone can go home walks towards me. Although I hear the sirens, I don't hesitate and shoot both of them.

Around the corner comes the sound of people whimpering. There are more lying in wait, but as I walk toward them, I hear "POLICE! DROP YOUR WEAPON!"

As I turn the corner, I see three women in blue scrubs, huddled together. They shake and, as the police close in on me, all I can think of is Marla.

"This all happened because you didn't save her. One job. You could have fucking helped my fiancé," I whisper as I bring the gun to my mouth, shoving it in and paying attention to my angle. I want to die in one shot, not after years of suffering.

As a policeman turns the corner, he lowers his gun, and his partner behind him holds his aim on me. I cock my eyebrow, and picture my dove's face, before I take my final shot. Blackness surrounds me, but this time I welcome it. I will spend an eternity looking for Marla. I'll find her again and we will live wrapped in each other's souls.

Thirty

Marla

When I open my eyes, I find myself no longer in the bathtub, although there aren't pearly white gates or a ring of fire, either. I'm lying on what appears to be a forest floor, except the trees don't have leaves. The decay that covers the branches as they twist at awkward angles is haunting.

Dampness sinks into my clothes and as I pull myself into a sitting position, I look up and the sky is red and orange. The air is hazy with no sun or moon. There are thundering noises in the distance, but silence encompasses me as I rise to my feet.

My body aches for Sebastian. What I did tore us apart and it's my fault that I'll never find him again. I love him so fucking much. If I could have had just a moment away from the darkness that intertwined within my mind, I might have stayed.

My heart doesn't hurt, but apprehension fills me. The fear that grips me surprises me, I hadn't expected it. I walk through the dense trees, and the sound of rustling leaves surrounds me until I reach a path. I follow it for a while, the hairs on the back of my neck standing on end as I feel the weight of someone's gaze on me. I turn my head over my shoulder, but no one is there. The path is empty but the feeling doesn't go away.

Heavy footsteps follow me as I continue to walk, I look back once more only to be greeted with more shadows and no movement. Fear pulses through my veins, and my head whips around to see but nothing is here. In my quest to find the source of the eyes, presence, and noise, I collide with something.

No, someone. I observe the person in front of me. He can't be any older than I am. His eyes whip around the trail we are on, filled with trepidation, and I wonder if he feels it too.

"Who are you?" I whisper.

His head swivels quickly as he continues to look around us. His eyes finally focus on mine. "I'm Sid. Who are you?"

"Marla. Is this hell?" I ask, pushing myself to continue walking to follow this person, even though I don't know where we are going.

"No, I don't think so. I feel like I'm in a weird video game. Like I was spawned over there in the woods, and now am supposed to figure out what the goal is." He isn't wrong, but it would be the worst video game that ever existed.

"Have you seen other people?" He slows his pace so I can walk beside him. "Not yet. You are the first, but there have been dark shadows following me."

I have seen no shadows yet. Despite my searching gaze, there are no signs of them anywhere. Upon reaching a bridge, my eyes automatically glance downward, hoping for a tranquil waterway, only to be met by a desolate expanse of jagged rocks. A person is looking over the edge as we reach them. She lifts her head from looking down and walks towards us.

"Who are you?" she asks. This is going to get redundant.

"I'm Marla, this is Sid. We woke up in the forest. Who are you?"

She seems taken aback by my abruptness. "Rhile. Where are we?"

"What is the last thing both of you remember? What were you doing before you came here? It's going to help us figure out what the fuck is going on." I lean my back against the railing of the bridge and look at both of them. Redness covers her cheeks and I realize she might be embarrassed.

"I got into my bathtub, took a bunch of pills, and cut open my wrists, then I woke up here. So, who wants to share next?" Looking down, I see no scars from what I did, but I know this isn't Earth, unless I'm in one seriously messed up dream.

No one says anything for what feels like forever. I can vaguely make out large dark shadows in the woods. I don't know what they are, but fear fills me.

"I wrapped a rope around my neck and walked off the ledge of our barn. I couldn't deal with the darkness anymore," Sid whispers. I see what we have in common, and I look to Rhile.

"I took all the pills the doctor gave me. They kept trying to fix me and nothing was working."

"Alright, so from what I can tell, we are in some sort of space that people go to when they kill themselves. Can anyone else see the twenty-foot black shadow coming out of the forest?" They both look, but I can tell they haven't seen it when they look back at me. They both shake their heads.

Great, we're in some sort of weird reality with something chasing me. "Let's keep walking. Maybe we'll figure out something, or find someone else." Instinct kicks in, telling me I needed to get out of here.

After what feels like days, we reach a trio of cabins. I've heard screaming, yelling, and a lot of crying along the walk, but we are no closer to understanding what is happening.

"I'm going to go knock on the door." Sid grabs my arm, but I shake out of his grasp. "We need to know what's going on."

I stalk towards the door and knock. After a few minutes, it opens and a large man walks out on the stoop. He's dressed in what looks like a robe, but also jeans. I'm confused as I look into his dark green eyes. I feel at peace for a minute, but fear resumes its place in my heart.

"Hi, I'm Marla. We're just wondering if you know what this place is?"

He walks back into his cabin, and I think he's going to close the door, but he reappears. From the corner of my eye, I can see two more people coming from the other cabins dressed the same as him.

"Usually, we don't do introductions or guides. This isn't summer camp, but never has someone come to our cabins, either. We've tried to give small bits of information, but over time we found our presence caused more harm than good."

"I'm Berimund, and these are Giso and Tanco. You are in Cavum Terra, you are here because you killed yourself. We don't like to ruin the surprise, but you aren't at peace, nor are you alone. Time moves quickly here, and you will have to fight."

I take in his words. Looking over my shoulder, I realize that the shadows have become more humanoid looking, and that should be my next question. "So, it's not summer?"

"We don't have seasons here, but if I check my log." He pulls out a phone-looking device. "You've been here for six years already compared to Earth."

My mind explodes. I don't understand how simply walking this far equates to time moving that quickly.

"I've been here for a millennium and time really goes by slowly," he tells me. I bite my lip.

"Do you know if my mother is here?" I look around.

"No, you killed her. Any more questions?"

"What are the shadow-human things?" Sid pipes up from behind me. I was getting to it, but at least my mother isn't gracing my presence after death.

"It's already going to be terrifying, just tell them Berimund." He shakes his head and lifts his shoulders. Giso sighs heavily. She has beautiful golden locks that fall around her shoulders, her face is kind and her violet eyes put me at ease until she talks.

"The shadow-human-things will form into full demons. You won't be able to see each others. They haunt and fight each one of you. You thought taking your life would end the demons in your mind, but they followed you here. You can never escape them."

That is fucking terrifying, and before I can ask another question, she smiles lightly and they return to their cabins.

"Well, fucking hell, that's great. What are we going to do?" Sid asks as he looks behind himself.

"Fight, I guess, but I'm going to rest before we walk more." I turn away from him to walk to a large thick tree. Leaning my back against it, I sit on the ground.

As I look down the path that we came from I can see three distinct-looking monsters. One is sky-high tall, and thin, dark tendrils fall from its form, like long fingers that could wrap around you and never let you go. It is the least formed, which leads me to believe that it will get more frightening with time.

The second demon monster is smaller, but has fangs. It's not like any vampire I've seen in movies. The bold purple skin makes its features stand out, and the orange eyes seem to beat like a heartbeat.

I close my eyes and lean my head on my knees. If I had depression and anxiety in my last life, then these slightly make sense, but I don't know what the other one is.

Lifting my head, I look out over the hills where they stand. The third is tall and light blue. Hand-like features hang at their sides, the eyes are black as night, and as they walk closer, the colours change through the trees. It's camouflaging against each background it walks through.

My breath catches in my throat. Life wasn't the worst thing I was living. At least they were in my head there. Now I have to face them head-on alone. Sebastian crosses my mind again. For the billionth time, I know it was self-induced, but the pain of leaving him behind is the only thing that I know is real here, and I hang onto it tightly to keep myself half sane.

"Can you see yours?" Sid asks me. Both of them have slumped down against the tree with me.

"Yeah, they are fucking terrifying. I don't know how I'm supposed to fight them. I wasn't able to fight it in life."

"Me either, but at least I only see one giant beast." He sounds hopeful, and I think I'm more fucked than I thought.

"I have two, but they aren't huge. I don't know what I'll do either, Marla." Rhile grips my hand and I'm reminded of Jess, who I didn't even ask about, but since she didn't pull the trigger, I'm assuming she isn't here.

We all sit and watch people run, flashes of colour from their shirts or pants as they run from the demons that are tracking them. My ears fill with sorrowful cries, and tortured whimpers surround us, as do screams of horror. It will be something that takes a while to get used to.

It feels like months, but it could be years since that day at the tree when we learned the truth about where we are. Sometimes I run into Sid or Rhile, but rarely. I've made some other friends, but I spend most of my time running. The first week, my demons cornered me. Up close they are even more terrifying and the way their voices can lure you to salvation or destroy you is haunting.

"Your soul is ours," they often tell me. It makes me feel like I never had a choice in the matter, that I would have never gotten the help because there wasn't any help for me. As if my fate was always to end up here, being tracked by the demons from my mind.

After an altercation with my camouflaging demon left me ripped to shreds, I healed within days. It means they can bring us within an inch of the end and wait for us to recover before we are healed enough to fight again. It's like dying a painful death over and over. Maybe it's exactly what I deserved. I did some shitty things on Earth, I broke the only person I've ever loved. The memory of Sebastian never leaves me. With each beat of my heart I'm reminded of his love, of the taco dates, of the way I felt laying on his chest.

I lay on the ground where I first came to this realm, under a set of trees whose branches look like they could eviscerate my skin. I know the monsters are close. I can feel them. The tallest one with the longest fingers can reach me from here, often planting thoughts inside my head, telling me I'm not good enough, and that I don't deserve to be here. Much like on Earth, my mind isn't a very nice place. I long for the day this ends, or I lose my mind completely.

"What in the fucking hell is this horseshit?" I hear someone yell from behind the trees. I leap up and follow the cursing voice because it might be him. Sebastian might be here.

Sometimes my demons like to play tricks and lead me to his voice, but as I continue through the brush, feeling the agony of the thorns that are as big as my hand rip through my skin, I make it to a different clearing. At the bottom of the hill, there is a set of trees that aren't as distorted as the ones I just left. The air leaves my lungs as I stare at the figure on the ground. I'm inching closer, terrified it's a trick. I lean down to look into his face.

"Sebastian?"

Thirty-One

Sebastian

She is exactly as I remember. Her hair is a little ruffled and messy and she seems to be bleeding. As I look up into her hazel eyes I know it's her. "I told you I'd always find you, my dove."

She crawls to me, collapsing onto my chest, and I wrap my arms around her. I lay on my back as her grip tightens around my neck, her lips connect with mine. I return her kiss just as fiercely.

"I love you." The words from her lips are everything I've been needing. Everything will be just fine, I think. As I look around, I wonder how true that is, but as long as I'm with her, nothing else matters.

"I'm so fucking sorry, Sebastian. I just couldn't tell you how I was feeling, and I needed to escape my mind. Wait, how are you here?"

"What do you mean? I died. I'm here. Isn't that how this works?"

Her eyes dart around the area we are in. "Can you see your shadow demons yet?"

I glance around but see nothing but a hazy red and orange sky. "I assumed this was hell." I've done enough bad things to make it here on a one-way ticket.

"No, it's not. This is the Cavum Terra. You come here when you kill yourself. It's been fucking crazy, scary, and I've just been holding onto the pain I felt for losing you." I think over my actions, remembering getting the gun from Mr. Sharp and what came next. I purse my lips and nod.

"Well? What did you do?" I roll her over onto her back, while I stay on my side to stroke her hair, my thumb caressing her cheek and wiping away the tears that have fallen.

"The night I came home and you were gone, my heart was done for. My mind couldn't function. After I laid with you for days, time ceased to exist, but I had to have a purpose in my life. So I called Mr. Sharp. He gave me gun lessons and taught me how to shoot with accuracy. The following day, I drove to the mental health centre. Wait, is Jess here?" Her eyes close and she shakes her head.

"Anyone who's died naturally or was killed isn't here. I don't get to see my best friend again, or my grandparents, but at least I exist in a place without my mother."

My lip curls on one side in a half smile. My heart breaks for her, but I'm glad she isn't eternally damned to her mother.

"You laid with me after? What did you do at the mental health centre?" Her eyes open and she looks at me.

"I did. I pulled you out of the tub, brought you to bed and laid with you until I felt you would probably be mad at me. Then I buried you in the backyard with your favourite flowers." Her hand on my cheek brings me closer to her. Out of the corner of my eye, I notice a tall, wide shadow. As I attempt a closer look, nothing is there.

"They'll be coming for you soon. Tell me what you did at the mental health centre and then we'll find somewhere safe."

"Who's coming, Marla?"

"The demons from your mind. Whatever you suffered with mentally on Earth follows you here. I have three demons. I don't know what the third is, even after all this time, but it likes to taunt me. It often uses your voice to remind me of losing you. It camouflages to fit in everywhere, so I never know where it is. Anxiety and depression lurk around just as much, but that one just never leaves me be. I won't be able to see yours and you won't be able to see mine."

Well, fuck. Maybe hell would have been better, but I don't give a fuck as long as I can help her fight her monsters here for eternity.

"I wasn't diagnosed with anything. How will I know what mine is?" I ask her. She runs her hand over my chest and her touch ignites my desire for her. Love pumps through my veins, I've missed her so fucking much.

"I don't know. I only have the two diagnoses, so whatever was in your head without you knowing. What did you do?"

"Interesting. The mental health centre failed you, so when I got there, I killed a bunch of the workers, and the doctors, and I would have continued, but the police came. So I shot myself." Her face falls. I thought this was what she would have wanted, what we needed to avenge her death.

"I'm sorry that I knocked the dominos over to have you end your life. It was never my intention, but I'm glad you found me. I've missed you."

"I did my best to save you. It's all I've ever wanted to do for you." She kisses my lips, her fingers trail along my neck, and I grip her tightly.

"We have to move. I don't know if we can find cover, but we can try. There are many people here and three lords, or royals. I don't know, I've never figured it out."

The information means nothing to me. I don't care what I'm up against. As long as she is beside me, I'll be able to face anything. When she gets up, I follow her through the clearing to a secluded area filled with trees. The branches are sharp, like nails sticking out of wood, brushing against our skin and breaking it open. "Do you get hurt a lot here?"

"Yeah, we seem to heal quickly. Your monsters will want to take you to the edge of your life and let you heal to go for another round."

I wince, thinking about what she's had to go through while waiting for me to arrive. I grind my teeth, thinking about the torture I'll have to see her go through while we are here.

"I met a seasoned couple. They didn't start as a couple, but they came in at the same time. They said if you don't want to fight, you can run away and if you hide well enough, then you won't have to be in battle as much."

Honestly, battle doesn't seem like the worst thing. I could enjoy the battle, but wish I could fight her monsters instead of mine.

I swipe my finger over her arm, clearing the blood and tasting her just as I remember. She reaches for my shirt and pulls me closer to her, then her hand snakes up to my neck to pull me down. My mouth goes to hers and I kiss her fiercely, capturing her moans with my tongue. I peel off her shirt, breaking our kiss, and feast my eyes on her beautiful tits. Lowering my tongue to her skin, I trace circles around her nipples as she pulls on my hair.

"We probably shouldn't do this. We have to get further to hide," she whispers, but I don't give a fuck.

"I've hungered for you for what feels like forever."

I lower us to the soft ground. Although damp, it's not scratchy, like the surrounding trees. She peppers my face with kisses as I pull off my jeans and rip hers down. Finding her clit with my thumb, I rub circles around it until she is quivering.

"Please," she breathes.

"What do you want, my dove?"

"You. Your cock. Please. It's been so fucking long." Without needing any more words, I sink into her. Sliding in slowly, I look into her eyes when I'm buried deep inside of her. As I adjust to her heat that I've missed, her perfect cunt grips my dick and I fuck her. My grip digs into her hips as I lower my head, taking her nipple in my mouth to suck on as I thrust into her. As she milks my cock, I lose my mind and growl into her neck, biting her as I fill her with my come.

After we finish, we lay like that for a few minutes, my weight on her as I catch my breath. She kisses my forehead and we pull apart to redress.

"That was fucking perfect. I missed you, but I'm pretty sure I said that," she says as we stand. She leads me to continue walking through the forest.

"You can tell me the same thing over and over and I'd never bore of your words. My existence has only ever been to be with you, to do my best to save you. Now that our souls are intertwined, and our hearts beat together, I think we can make it through," I tell her. I do my best to think of what type of monster may follow me, but I can't place what it might be other than anger.

"We'll make it through. They told me my soul is theirs, but I won't break down with you here. I'm stronger with you by my side, holding my hand, and I'll be able to handle whatever happens."

"Of course we will, my dove. I'll never leave your side again, we do this together forever."

A Note from the author

Suicide is a serious thing. If you or anyone you know feels like you can't continue living? Please reach out, to a friend, an internet friend, or anyone. 9-8-8 is a national suicide crisis line that you can access to talk to. I've been there more than once. Reach out, because you are needed here.

Self-harm is a silent battle that not everyone faces. I understand that when everything feels overwhelming, it can feel like an old friend, or you are feeling so numb you just want to feel something. But we'll never reach that first high again.

Thank you for reading. If you could drop a review or rating, I would be forever grateful. Also, shit happens, so do typos. If you catch one, don't hesitate to slip into my DMs.

Acknowledgements

To anyone who reads this book, I appreciate your time and interest.

My betas, I'm sorry for breaking you and I love you.

To my editing team, I'm thankful for everything you catch and help with.

The hype girl squad, thanks for always being there for me. I wouldn't be where I am without your love and support.

Sarren, Kim, Kym, Elisabeth, Tara, W.L Brooks, and so many others. Thank you for being the family that won't leave me. I love ya'll.

To the ARC readers- ya'll the MVPs. Thank you for you're time and effort.

To my best friend who helped edit pieces out of context, I'd be lost without you.

Also By Tanya Lynn

Mask of Broken Things
The Last Broken Piece
Branches of Betrayal
Branches of Intimacy
Stealing His Sunshine
If He Wanted To, He Wood

About the Author

Tanya has dreamed about being an author her entire life, and continues to work toward making a career out of it. Tanya lives in Canada with two incredible kids and a high-maintenance cat.

Subscribe to her newsletter, she doesn't spam and barely remembers to send one monthly. You can find her on social media through the QR code or her website. www.tanyalynn100.ca